Inception

By Gary Hope

"Inception," by Gary Hope. ISBN 978-1-63868-096-3 (softcover); 978-1-63868-097-0 (hardcover).

Published 2023 by Virtualbookworm.com Publishing Inc., P.O. Box 9949, College Station, TX , 77842, US.

This book is dedicated to all those who think nobody cares

To all those who are looking for love, and

To all those who think that life is passing them by . . .

It's not

ONE

THE WEDDING FOR NIAMH AND MARK was set for 3:00 Sunday afternoon. That way everyone could get home from church, have something to eat, and change clothes for the biggest wedding the little village of Dungloe had ever seen. Everyone in the entire town was invited, as well as some friends from Dublin, Burtonport, Galway, and across the ocean in North Carolina. Ailen, the richest man in town, who also owned most of the profitable businesses, declared Sunday a holiday and vowed to throw the biggest party the county of Donegal had ever seen. Maybe the biggest party all of Ireland had ever seen.

The groom, Mark, and his soon-to-be bride, Niamh, had been searching for each other for over three hundred years. When they finally overcame all the obstacles and found each other, it was as though the Sea Gods of Tir-na-nOg had blessed them for eternity. Everyone in this part of Ireland knew they were perfect for each other. But most importantly Niamh and Mark knew they were perfect for each other. Ever since that fateful day on the sea cliff outside Burtonport, where they met and kissed for the first time, they knew—they absolutely knew they had found their magical and eternal partners. Sometimes, love is like that.

Niamh had been raised here in the rural villages of Ireland. This was her home. She and her daughter were suddenly left alone several years ago when her husband was killed in a fishing accident at sea. She went through several dark and lonely years which changed in an instant the day she met Mark on the cliff.

Mark was not a local. He had moved here to the backroads of Ireland to get away from some personal troubles and failures in his hometown, Winston-Salem, North Carolina. After a few months of living in Dungloe, he felt as if he was reborn. He felt as if he was indeed Irish and belonged there. The day he met Niamh at the cliff cemented his feelings and he was locked into the life he had always dreamed about. It took Niamh and him a while to connect but neither of them could imagine a life without the other. It's hard for most of us to imagine one kiss being so defining, so prophetic, and so incredible. But to them, it was as natural as breathing.

Ailen, the owner of several businesses in town, including the pub where the biggest of the parties would be held, also had a home on the Atlantic coast a few miles from town. He now lived in Winston-Salem, N.C. with his new wife, the beautiful Gabriella. Ailen trusted Mark to run his businesses in Dungloe and Mark had never disappointed him. Ailen and Mark were not just business owner and employee. They were friends, companions, and brothers. Each trusted the other with everything. They had a special bond that is hard to find in this world. But they had it.

The wedding on Sunday would be officiated by Mark's friend, GC, the pastor of the local Baptist church in Dungloe. Even though the population of Ireland is 95% Catholic, GC had a small but loyal congregation, of which Mark was a member. Niamh grew up Catholic but had never been a regular churchgoer. She immediately connected with Mark's friend GC and agreed to have the wedding at the Baptist church. Everyone in Dungloe, Catholic and Baptist alike, love GC and his wife Layla. The entire town and countryside were buzzing with anticipation.

After the wedding, the largest of the parties would be held at the local pub that Ailen owned, and Mark managed. Actually, Mark did very little managing of the pub. He didn't need to because he had Eileen to manage it for him. Eileen was initially hired to be the head bartender however, she was so good and efficient, it didn't take long for Mark to figure out that she could run things better than he could. So, Mark's job now consisted of stopping by and asking Eileen how things were going, while he sipped his daily coffee or Guinness. Usually, Eileen didn't even answer him. She would just smile and walk away, which was fine with Mark.

Mark managed several other businesses for Ailen that required a lot of his time. The main headache he had now was the town's main restaurant. This restaurant had been in constant turnover since the woman who ran it efficiently for years had eloped and moved to Portugal with a man she met online. Her name was Claire. Anyone who ever met Claire would never forget her . . . that was certain! Since she left Dungloe, Mark had hired and fired several managers at the restaurant. It was his biggest headache by far. He even tried to talk Niamh into managing it after their wedding. She knew better. So, Mark would continue to work on the revolving door nature of this business. Not now . . . but after the wedding.

Today, the Friday before the wedding, was busy with everyone making plans for either the party that night, or the bigger party Saturday night or the massive after-wedding party on Sunday. Ailen, of course, was paying for everything. Mark and Niamh tried to reason with him, but he would not listen. That's the way Ailen was. So, extra kegs of Guinness were delivered along with crates of Jameson, all sorts of Irish delicacies, chocolates, meats, and anything else Ailen could think of. Everyone would be happy. Ailen would make sure of that.

Most brides would be nervous wrecks two days before their wedding. Not Niamh. She was never more sure of anything in her life. Her mother tried to get her to "highlight" her hair, but she would have nothing to do with that. Mark loved the color of her hair. He always told everyone that the slight tinge of red in her light brown hair complimented her green eyes as only an angel could have painted. Niamh would never change that. Her only concession with her mother was to wear the wedding gown her mother had worn on her wedding day all those years ago. It had to be altered a bit, but it was beautiful and sentimental. Everyone else was running on empty—Niamh was as satisfied, happy, and calm as anyone ever could be.

Mark was a bit nervous, not about the marriage, but that something might happen in the next two days to prevent the marriage: world war, atomic bomb, Martians invading. His mind wouldn't stop. All he wanted was Niamh. Forever, and ever, and ever. This would be Mark's second marriage. His first wife, in North Carolina, had deceived him, stolen his money, and run off with a scoundrel lawyer. All these circumstances are what caused him to move away and start a new life here in the northern, remote section of Ireland. The place he now considered his home.

However, even the happiest of days can sometimes have their own troubles. This morning as Mark was at the pub having his daily coffee with Eileen, the newest of his managers at the restaurant walked into the bar, stood at the doorway, and yelled at Mark, "I quit!" Then he turned around and walked out. No explanation, nothing other than he quit. It was stunning. Here, two days before the wedding, the manager of the restaurant where many of the festivities would be held had quit. Mark was absolutely stunned. He looked over the bar at Eileen, who said,

"I knew it. He was worthless. You should've never hired him."

Mark first stared at her, then back towards the empty door, then turned back to Eileen and questioned, "You knew he was worthless? Why didn't you say something?"

"I did say something. When you told me you were hiring him, I said, 'Really?'"

4

Mark answered, "You said, 'Really?' How is that warning me, Eileen?"

She picked up a glass from the washer and began drying it and answered, "Mark, you can ignore the reality, but you cannot ignore the consequences of ignoring that reality." As he was trying to understand what that meant, she walked to the other side of the bar to sign an invoice from a delivery man. At that moment, his cell phone rang. It was Ailen asking if everything was good.

"No, Ailen, it's not good. The restaurant manager just quit with no notice. Who's going to run the place for the next two days? This is a disaster!" Ailen had no answer. He was as shocked as Mark. All he could say was,

"You'll figure it out. You always do. I've got to run. Talk to you later."

Mark sat staring into his cup of cold coffee, with his mind whirling. *"How am I going to get through the party tonight? And the party tomorrow night? And the after-wedding party?"*

"Claire."

He looked up and Eileen was staring at him with her eyebrows arched. He said, "What?"

"Claire, that's what."

"What do you mean, Claire?"

Eileen said, "Hire her back. She's the best you've ever had. Problem solved."

"In case you've forgotten, she lives in Portugal now with her husband. Or had that small piece of information slipped your mind?"

Eileen smiled and answered, "No she doesn't. She lives in Galway now and she's not married anymore. Call her, Mark. I know you two had your differences, but you also know she's the best person for the job. Do it!"

"You're not the boss here, Eileen."

"Mark, do it! Call her now." As she said that, she held out a card with a phone number on it. She continued holding the card until he took it from her. Then she said, "Now."

He held the card but truly didn't know what he should do. First, he wondered how Eileen always knew what he should do or think before he even knew himself. True, Claire was good at managing the restaurant, but the two of them could not get along. Complete opposites in everything, she was a huge thorn in his side. But Mark couldn't deny that she was very good at managing the restaurant. As he sat there thinking, Eileen poured him another cup of coffee and said, "The bottom line in life is that sometimes good things happen. Sometimes bad things happen. But, Mark, if you don't take a chance, nothing will happen."

TWO

"HELLO."

"Claire?"

"Yes . . . who is this?"

"It's Mark, calling from the pub in Dungloe."

"Mark who?"

"What do you mean, 'Mark who?'"

"You could be anybody."

"How many men in Dungloe, with American accents, named Mark, would be calling you?"

"I have lots of friends in Dungloe."

At this point, Mark was so frustrated he nearly hung up the phone. "Well, I'm not one of them. I'm your former boss calling to see if you're interested in coming back to Dungloe to manage the restaurant. Are you?"

Claire waited a few seconds before answering, because . . . well, because she was Claire. Then she said, "Maybe."

Mark looked up from the phone and Eileen said to him, "You need her, Mark. Don't let her get to you."

Mark spoke back into the phone, "I need an answer now, Claire. Either you do want to come back, or you don't. Which is it?"

Several seconds of silence passed before she answered, "What will you pay me to come rescue you from your trouble?"

He wanted to slam the phone down so hard that it would shatter! But then he remembered the wedding, and the parties, and Niamh, and most importantly right now, Eileen, who was staring fiercely at him with her hands on her hips. So, he answered, "Same as you were making when you left."

Silence. Then, "I want a raise."

"A raise? For what? You haven't done anything to deserve a raise. That's preposterous!"

"Okay, then good luck finding someone, Mark. Nice talking to you." Only, she didn't hang up. She held the phone in silence. Mark held his phone in silence. The only difference being that Mark had Eileen staring a hole in him like a blowtorch through his soul. They both held their phones in silence, a contest of wills, and stubbornness. It was a contemptuous friendship they had with each other.

Finally, Mark relented and asked, "How much?"

"You decide what's fair, Mark. I trust you."

At last, she had said something that didn't anger him. "Okay, when can you get here? I'm in a little jam right now."

She answered, "I'm here now. I'll be at the restaurant in about twenty minutes."

Mark wanted to ask, *"Twenty minutes?"* But he didn't. He wanted to ask, *"How?"* But he didn't. All he had to do was look in Eileen's eyes and he knew the answer to those questions. Without saying anything else, he hung up his phone and stared at Eileen. She gave him a crooked looking smile and he said, "You knew all along, didn't you?"

Eileen now smiled brightly and said, "Yeah, Mark, I knew. You were the only one who didn't know."

Mark said, "She told me she'd be at the restaurant in twenty minutes. How?"

Before he could finish his question, Eileen answered, "She's at my apartment. I invited her down yesterday. I knew we needed her, even if you didn't."

He wanted to ask, *"How? Why? When? Where?"* And *"Seriously?"* But he knew better. And he knew she was right. He needed Claire. Then, before he could think clearly again, Eileen took the cold cup of coffee away from him and poured him a shot of Jameson's. That, he needed.

* * *

Mark figured he should walk down to the restaurant and break the news about Claire to the staff. They all knew Claire and had worked for her and with her in the past. Mark wasn't entirely sure how they'd take the news of her coming back. As he walked in the door of the restaurant, he noticed it was about half full of regular customers, but there was no staff to be seen. No waitresses. No one at the cashier's desk. No busboys. No one at all. He started walking to the kitchen and heard voices. Claire!?! He distinctly heard her voice. He opened the kitchen door and there she was: dressed in her ankle-length dress, her red hair piled up in a bun on top of her head, wearing no makeup at all, and giving instructions like she was a drill sergeant.

When she saw him, she stopped mid-sentence and asked, "What do you want? Can't you see we're busy here?" Poor Mark had enough common sense to do the right thing and quietly backed out the door. Claire was back! They had always had an awkward relationship. Sometimes she acted as though she hated him and, sometimes she acted like she was flirting with him.

Claire reminded him of the quintessential poster girl of the Amish country back in the United States. She always wore long dresses down to her ankles, always had her red hair tied in a bun on top of her head, and never wore makeup. Well, almost never. There was that one time, years ago before Mark ever knew he'd find Niamh, when there was a party at Ailen's house on the coast. Everyone there had way too much to drink, including Mark. The house was packed, and Mark knew fewer than half the people there. After a few minutes, he noticed a tall, long-legged woman in high-heels, and a short skirt. She had long flowing hair and thick eyelashes.

Mark was transfixed by her beauty. He asked her to dance, and she accepted. They slow-danced to several songs, becoming more and more entranced with each other and with the moment. After the first song, she pulled back from Mark and looked directly in his eyes and he kissed her. A long, passionate kiss that had everyone in the room staring. They were staring, not because of the passionate nature of the kiss, but because it was Mark kissing his arch enemy, Claire. Yes, Claire had dressed for the party so that no one recognized her. She'd traded her normal Amish costumes for some Playgirl outfit that would have embarrassed Hugh Hefner. Mark fell for her hook, line, and sinker.

After the song, Mark's new love excused herself to visit the restroom and Mark went to the bar for a drink. He was very excited. The bartender asked him, "How does she kiss?"

The question seemed a bit awkward, but Mark answered truthfully, "Best I've had in quite some time. By the way, do you happen to know her name? She didn't tell me."

The bartender backed up suddenly and said, "You don't know her name?"

"No." Mark answered, "We were a bit too involved to be asking questions—if you know what I mean."

The bartender handed Mark his pint of Guinness and said, "That's Claire."

Mark could have sworn the bartender was speaking German, or French, or maybe even Pig-Latin . . . certainly not English, because it sounded like he said, "Claire."

He stood stunned for a few seconds and the bartender repeated, "Yeah, that's Claire. Your Claire. She cleans up pretty nice, doesn't she?"

Mark wasn't sure if he stood there a few seconds or a few years. He lost all concept of reality when someone tapped his shoulder. He turned around to find that the beauty he'd just danced with and kissed so passionately was standing there looking at him and smiling. She said, "Want another dance?"

Mark was stunned. It was Claire. He now recognized her voice. How could this have happened? He asked, "Claire?"

"Yes."

"It's you?"

"Yes, Mark, who did you think I was?"

His head was spinning so bad, all he could do was turn and walk away. As he started walking out of the room, everyone stopped and was staring at what happened, Claire yelled out, "No! I will not go to bed with you and don't ever ask me that question again."

Needless to say, the two of them had a long, hard time forgetting that night. No one knew who was telling the truth: Mark or Claire. But it made fine gossip for months and months. And now she was back.

ThREE

NIAMH WAS PROBABLY THE CALMEST PERSON in all of Dungloe. From the first time she met Mark on the seaside cliff, she knew he was the man for her. He was the man who would make her happy. How did she know? She couldn't explain. She just knew. Maybe it was his gentle and caring demeanor. Or maybe the way he looked into her hypnotic green eyes. Or, most likely, it was the way she felt when they kissed that first time, with the wind whipping so wildly about them. She remembers telling him how her name is derived from the daughter of the Sea God, Manannan. She is a beautiful princess who rides a white horse and comes from Tir-na-nOg, 'The Land of the Young,' which is a supernatural realm of everlasting youth, beauty, health, abundance, and joy, where three hundred years passes in what seems like three weeks."

She remembered the look on Mark's face as he heard this tale. How he was so completely captivated and truly seemed to believe every word of it. Then she kissed him. She hadn't planned on kissing him. She had never kissed a man first before. It was as if the Sea God herself had prescribed her actions. Then, Mark kissed her back. And that was all it took for them both to be utterly, completely, and irrevocably joined together. Oh, it took a while for them to overcome some difficulties. But they did. Now a life's dream was only two days away. Niamh was the happiest woman in the world, just as Mark felt he was the happiest man in the world.

Niamh's first husband had died several years earlier in a fishing accident at sea. A steel cable had snapped and when it recoiled, Niamh's husband was caught in the backlash. The cable cut him in half. Niamh's daughter, Ennis, was only a toddler at the time. Niamh didn't know then if she would ever recover from this tragic event. The only good thing from that time was that her husband's company had a large life insurance policy for their employees. Niamh was suddenly a very rich woman, at least by rural Irish standards. She would certainly never have to work again.

In the last several months Niamh had taken to playing her fiddle with a group of friends at local pubs. Usually there would be one or two fiddle players, one or two guitar players, and maybe a tambourine player on occasion. The cast changed from week to week, which was normal for pubs in Ireland. Niamh loved playing. It soothed her mind and released feelings she had inside. When she finally found Mark again, she was playing with several friends at a pub in Burtonport, a neighboring village. She had her eyes closed as she was playing a song. When she opened her eyes, Mark was standing in front of her, four feet away. She jumped into his arms and their magical life tour began.

Her daughter, Ennis, loved Mark as well. She loved listening to his stories of growing up in North Carolina and how life was in the rural south. Niamh was never quite sure if Mark's stories were entirely true, but Ennis loved them and that was what mattered. They had picked out a house to live in after the wedding, which was located on the coast near Ailen's house. Though not as big as Ailen's, it was still very nice with a view of the sea where several small islands lay off the coast.

Tonight, Friday, Ailen had reserved the pub for his own special party for Mark and Niamh. He had invited all their friends, including Mark's best friend, other than Ailen, who was named James. James, which in the Irish language is pronounced "Jims," owned a bar in Burtonport, which is also where the cliff was located where Mark and Niamh first met. This nice, family pub is where Niamh's small band played regularly. When Ailen went on one of his trips to America, Jims became Mark's best friend and most trusted confidant. They were more like father/son, whereas Mark and Ailen were more like older brother/younger brother.

Eileen had everything set up for the big party. Flowers were everywhere, streamers were hanging, and tables of food were spread around the pub. Of course, Guinness was also flowing in unlimited quantities. Mark had even trimmed his hair a bit and thinned out his goatee. He offered to cut them even more, but Niamh liked his hair a bit long and thought he looked more Irish with his straggly goatee.

Niamh, of course, didn't have to change anything. She was a natural beauty with her light brown hair, tinged with red, and those green eyes that had cast a spell on many a man, young and old, in County Donegal. Niamh was the kind of woman that would probably never win a beauty contest; but every man at the contest would be wishing to be with her instead of any woman on stage. The only woman at the party who came near her beauty was Ailen's wife, the beautiful Gabriella.

During his first trip to Winston-Salem, Ailen met Gabriella. They were introduced to each other and had two incredible dates. And then, just like that, they married! She was from Costa Rica but had lived in Winston-Salem nearly her entire life. She even had a slight southern twang in her voice. Everything about her was gorgeous. She and Ailen seemed as happy as any two people Mark had ever known. He knew that he and Niamh would have the same type of love and life as well.

Mark arrived at the pub before Niamh. He wanted to make sure everything was in order. When he walked in, Eileen waved him over to the bar and said, "What are you doing here so early? Didn't think I could manage the big night by myself?" She did not look happy. Mark was trying to think of something to say that would not make her mad. He failed.

"No," he stammered, "I was just walking by and thought I'd stop in and say hello . . . that's all."

"Mark, it would be best if you don't start out the night by lying. Then, it would be even better if you went home and changed that awful looking shirt you're wearing. What were you thinking, man?"

Mark looked down at his shirt that he ordered from Amazon especially for this night, and said, "What?"

"What?" Exclaimed Eileen, "Jesus, Mary, and Joseph, can you believe that shirt he's wearing, Conner?" She looked toward the old man sitting at the bar, listening to their conversation. Conner mumbled a few Gaelic words that were unintelligible to everyone at the bar, except Eileen.

Mark asked, "What did he say?"

"You don't want to know! Now get out of here and don't come back till you have Niamh with you. And, for the love of God, Mark—change that shirt!"

Mark really wanted a Guinness, but he followed orders and walked out of the bar. He started walking back towards his home and he soon passed Mrs. Rigby coming out of a butcher shop. He stopped in front of her and said, "Good afternoon, Mrs. Rigby, I hope you're well and planning on coming to the pub tonight for the big party." His goal was to ask her what she thought of his shirt. But before he could ask her that question, she answered,

"Aye, I sure am. We're really looking forward to it. But shouldn't you be getting home, Mark, and change your clothes? You don't want to be late for your own party, now do you?" She smiled and patted him on the arm as he she turned to walk away.

He did have the common sense to cross the street, on his way home, so he wouldn't walk in front of the restaurant where Claire was now working. No sense in tempting fate.

Niamh was dressed and watching her daughter do some schoolwork. It really didn't matter what Niamh wore, no one would notice. Her emerald eyes, red-tinged hair, and beautiful smile were all anyone ever saw. She found her fiddle and put it in the case, so she could carry it to the pub tonight. She knew several of her friends would be there and they would certainly play a few songs, as is the custom in every pub in Ireland. Her mother and father were coming by to pick her up so they could all go to the pub together.

They arrived a few minutes early so they could spend some time with their granddaughter, Ennis, who was excited to see them. Niamh's dad immediately started playing with Ennis, and her mother went in the kitchen to talk with her daughter. They first hugged and nearly started crying. Niamh's parents loved Mark and were very happy for their daughter. They knew how difficult things had been since Niamh's first husband had died.

Niamh asked her mother, "Ma, you and Dad have been so happy for all these years. Is there anything you can tell me that will help Mark and me find what you and Dad have?"

Niamh's mother never hesitated as she answered, "Honey, I've found that the recipe for a perfect marriage is this: two times a week we go to a nice pub or restaurant, have a little beverage, good food, and companionship. He goes on Tuesdays, and I go on Fridays." Before Niamh could respond, her mother burst out laughing and continued, "Don't worry, honey. You'll figure it out. You love each other and that's the most important thing. Trust me."

"I do, Ma. I do. Thanks."

FOUR

THE PUB FILLED UP EARLY and then spilled outside and down the streets. Eileen had set up tables and chairs down the sidewalk, which the police would not have normally allowed . . . but tonight was different. Jims had come over from Burtonport, which was only about eight miles away, and had brought old Conner with him. No one really knew how old Conner was. He could be anywhere from fifty to seventy, it was anyone's guess. No one really knew if he could speak English either, all they ever heard from him was Gaelic. But what everyone did know was that old Conner loved to drink. He could drink all day and all night, while he spoke in gibberish no one could understand, while he was drooling all over his shirt and pants.

Jims drove him over and would drive him back home afterward. He felt it was his duty. The Baptist minister, GC and his wife Layla, had also arrived, as had Ailen and Gabriella. Everyone was there waiting for the prospective bride and groom to arrive. Mark did change his shirt, only because he knew he'd never win an argument with Eileen. And he arrived with Niamh's family to cheers and congratulations from everyone. Old Conner hugged Niamh, spoke some unintelligible Gaelic phrases, then tried to hug Mark, who backed away and held his arm out to fend off any further advances.

After old Conner went back to his drink at the bar, Mark asked Niamh what Conner had said to her. "You don't want to know.

I could only understand half his words and I truly don't want to know the other half." It took nearly an hour for everyone to greet them, as they endured handshakes and hugs from the crowd. When it was finally over, Eileen told them that Ailen was waiting in the office to see them. Ailen hugged Niamh first, then hugged Mark for what seemed like ten minutes. After the tears had dried up, everyone went back out into the crowd for drinks and food. It was going to be a fun night.

After a few hours, Claire came into the pub and endured her own slobbering hug from old Conner. Then, she started looking around for Mark. Mark saw her arrive, still wearing her ankle length dress with her hair tied up in a tight bun on top of her head. He immediately started easing over towards the men's restroom. When she got closer, he went in the restroom to wait her out. As he started to check his phone for messages, the door opened, and Claire came in. "What are you doing, Claire, this is the men's room?"

"I know what room it is, Mark. I'm not stupid."

"Are you sure about that, Claire?"

As Mark asked that question, a gentleman opened one of the stalls and started to walk out the door. Claire stopped him and said, "Where do you think you're going?"

He was both stunned and half-afraid when he answered, "Out the door, to the party."

She stared at him and asked, "You're not going to wash your hands, for the love of Mary?" He backed towards the sink and quickly washed, while keeping an eye on Claire. When he dried off, she said, "Fine, now get out." He did. Mark looked at her but truly didn't know what to say. So, she continued, "I'll not let you kiss me again, Mark. Now would not be the time. You need to devote yourself to that kind, pretty girl out there. I won't ever mention this again and you need to forget me as well . . . do you understand?"

Mark's mind was whirling. Should he try and set her straight? Should he argue with her? Or just take the easy way out and say, 'Okay'? He chose that option. He looked directly in her eyes and said, "Okay, Claire." She stared back at him for about ten seconds, which seemed like ten minutes to Mark, then turned and walked out the door. Mark took about half a minute to collect himself, then he walked out as well. He scanned the crowd but didn't see Claire anywhere.

Niamh walked up to him and said, "She's gone." The rest of the night was spectacular. The Guinness was flowing, the food was delicious, and Niamh's friends joined her for about forty-five minutes of old Irish ballads. Ailen told stories of America. Eileen made sure people didn't get too rowdy. Old Conner babbled and drooled all over himself, and Mark loved every minute of it. But not nearly as much as he loved the green-eyed beauty playing the fiddle and staring back at him.

As with all parties, some people had too much to drink, and Eileen had to escort them out of the pub. Overall, however, it was a wonderful evening. Niamh's band played. Ailen tried to sing. Conner passed out with his head uncomfortably on the bar, and Mark wondered how he became the luckiest man in the world. After midnight, most folks started going home and Eileen's crew started cleaning up the mess. Ailen invited all the guests to take home any of the leftover food, and they did. Niamh left to put Ennis to bed and Mark started helping with the cleanup chores.

As they nearly completed everything, they realized old Conner was still asleep at the bar and Jims was not here. He had obviously forgotten about Conner when he left, so Mark volunteered to drive him home. They woke him enough to walk him to Mark's car, but he was asleep again before Mark could get in and start the engine. It only took about fifteen minutes for

Mark to make the drive over to Burtonport. The hard part now was waking Conner up again. When he finally did get him out of his seat, Mark noticed a large wet spot where old Conner had been sitting. He had wet his pants. Great! This is the spot where Niamh would be sitting after the wedding as they drove off for their honeymoon.

He finally got Conner into his house and dumped him into his own bed, fully clothed, soiled, and slobbering. He went back to his car, but the smell of Conner's mess was overwhelming. Mark decided to drive up to the cliffs, open the windows and doors, and let things air out a bit. He made the short drive to where he first kissed Niamh and it was still as windy as always. But there was a full moon to halfway illuminate things. Mark parked the car sideways to the prevailing wind and opened all windows and doors. The wind, which had originated in America had now blown across the ocean, unfettered, and unblocked, until it met the cliffs and Mark's car with the stench of old Conner.

Mark sat off to the side, against a rock, and watched the moon's reflection bounce off the vast ocean. He wished Niamh could be here with him to see it. He thought of their first trip up here when they kissed that magical day. He also thought of the many times he'd been there by himself when he was trying to find Niamh. These cliffs would forever be in his memory. He eased down a bit against the rock and closed his eyes to think about Niamh and their marriage. The next thing he knew, the sun was rising across the ocean and shining in his eyes. He'd fallen asleep. The wind had blown shut one of the doors on his car, but the smell was not nearly as bad as earlier, and the wet spot had completely dried. Time to go home.

When he arrived back in Dungloe, the pub hadn't opened yet, but the restaurant had . . . and Mark needed coffee badly. It never crossed his mind that Claire was back. He walked in and stumbled over to a large table, waiting for the waitress to come over and feed his coffee needs. Instead, Claire walked over and said, "What are you doing?"

He looked up and saw her staring at him and replied, "I just want some coffee, Claire. That's all. I don't want to argue with you."

"I understand how drunk, hungover people need coffee, but you can't sit at this table to ease your headache."

"And why not?"

"Because, Mark, this is a table for eight customers. I'm not going to let one person take up this space just to feed their hangover. You should act more like an adult than some ignorant teenager."

Mark did notice a party of five waiting up front for a table, but he did not want to admit that Claire was right. He sat there thinking, then said, "Okay. Do you have another table for me?"

"No."

"No?"

"No, Mark. Go on home before the police see you and put you in jail."

"Well, can you get me a coffee to go then? Please?"

Claire looked down at him and waited a few seconds before saying, "Alright, but get up from the table. You're hurting business." He rose and walked up to the front to wait for his coffee, standing next to the party of five. Then, Claire came to him holding his coffee and as she handed it to him, she said, "And, no, Mark, I'll not go to the movie with you tonight." Then she looked at the party of five and said, "This way folks. Sorry for the delay."

Mark wanted to throw the coffee in Claire's face, but the urge to drink it, settle his nerves, and ease his throbbing head won out. He turned and left, knowing she'd beaten him again. He made it home safely, but the coffee didn't. He spilled it as he got out of the car. He needed rest and sleep urgently and vowed to clean up the mess later today. This afternoon would be the biggest of the pre-wedding parties and he needed to be rested and ready.

He tried to sleep, but all he could think about was Claire. He consciously tried to think of Niamh and the wedding, or anything other than that Amish-looking she-devil. He finally gave up and took his shower, got dressed, and went to the pub to see Eileen, who should be there by now. When he walked in, she poured a cup of coffee for him before he even asked. She had that ability to always know what he wanted and what he was thinking before he ever said a word. He took a small sip, and it tasted like the best thing he'd ever put in his mouth. He almost relaxed, until Eileen told him, "Claire said that you were drunk and hungover. How could you do something like that? Don't you know how important this day is Mark?"

"I'm not drunk, and definitely not hungover, Eileen. How could you believe anything Claire says, anyway?"

"She also says you made a pass at her, but I don't think I believe that. It's not true, is it?"

"No, it's not true! Why did you tell me to hire her anyway? She's a devil!"

"Because she's a good devil, Mark. You know no one else can run the restaurant like she does. You know you'll never have to worry about anything, and that she'll turn a good profit. You know that." Mark did not want to admit any of that was right, even if it was. Before he could say anything else, Eileen topped off his coffee, patted his arm, and walked away. Today was going to be a long day.

FIVE

SATURDAY STARTED OUT A LITTLE BLUSTERY, overcast, and with a light mist in the air—not unusual for Ireland. After Mark had his coffee and a piece of banoffee, he picked up Niamh and they drove over to the Baptist church to have their pre-wedding meeting with GC, the preacher. GC had been Mark's good friend for a while and now he and his wife, Layla, were Niamh's friends as well. When they arrived, Layla and Niamh went back to another room, leaving GC and Mark alone in the office.

"So, Mark, are you ready?"

"You know I am. GC, I've been waiting for this day my entire life."

GC nodded. He knew of Mark's life as no one else did, except maybe Ailen. GC and Ailen both knew of Mark's past life in North Carolina, his failed marriage, and his move to Ireland; but only GC knew of the secret details of Mark's failed first marriage. It was something Mark had hidden well from everyone, except Niamh and GC. Mark's first marriage fell apart when his wife surprised him one day with the announcement that she didn't love him anymore; in fact, she had never loved him, and she wanted a divorce. He had no clue anything was wrong and was devastated.

He soon found out that his wife had been having an affair with a lawyer, with an unscrupulous reputation, for quite some time.

She had already started divorce proceedings when she confronted him that fateful day. After several weeks of trying to digest everything, Mark finally came up with his plan. Mark, whose real name at that time was Paul Alfred, decided to sell his small business, his house, his cars, and clean out his bank accounts, giving his scoundrel of a wife more than half the money, then leave for Ireland and start a new life. Only, he didn't tell her or anyone else of these plans.

Mark's (or Paul Alfred's) wife at the time didn't work and didn't have any assets of her own. Mark paid for the house and cars, and all the money in the bank was from his savings and investments. However, he knew his wife's lover had the reputation of being able to twist the truth and screw men out of everything. That's why Mark developed his plan. The day the divorce was finalized, he took more than half the money from all his assets and wrote a check to his now ex-wife. He then boarded a ship under a false name and left for Ireland.

He had no family left in North Carolina. He had no siblings and his parents had died years earlier in a car accident. He wanted a fresh start with no ties to his past, as far away from his ex-wife and her snake-of-a-lawyer boyfriend. He simply vanished, not owing a cent to anyone, anywhere. He had broken no laws. When he arrived in Ireland, he went to see a magistrate and had his name legally changed from Paul Alfred to Mark McCarty so no one could ever trace him down, especially his ex-wife and her boyfriend. The only thing left unsettled was a million-dollar life insurance policy Mark had bought several years earlier, under his name Paul Alfred. He didn't care about that, or what happened to it; he just wanted out.

GC and Niamh knew all of this. Ailen knew most of it, but no one else knew anything. Everyone else in Dungloe only knew of Mark McCarty and what a good man he was . . . and he was. He gave his ex-wife more than she deserved, and never broke any laws in America or Ireland. It took a few evenings for Niamh to assimilate all this information, but no matter what his name was, she knew she loved this man with all her heart, no matter what his past had been.

Now, GC only wanted to review the details of the wedding and see if Mark had any questions about how things would work. Layla and Niamh discussed the wedding dress, where the honeymoon would be, if Niamh was interested in having more children, and hundreds of other things. Niamh told her of the honeymoon they had planned down to Killarney and the Dingle peninsula, where they planned on doing some hiking. Layla knew how beautiful this area was and was extremely happy for her friend.

After the meeting, Mark dropped off Niamh at her house and he went home to change clothes and go back to the pub and help Eileen get ready for the big party.

* * *

Ailen had left nothing to chance. He had bought considerably more food than would ever be eaten. He had ordered more kegs of Guinness than could possibly be consumed (maybe) and had hired some teenagers to hang banners and streamers all over the pub and restaurant. Claire was not exactly happy with all this fuss, but she knew better than to ever argue with Ailen. He also ordered her to leave the restaurant early and go home to change clothes for the party. He didn't tell Mark of these plans—he didn't want to upset him too much.

Mark arrived at the pub in a gaudy-looking, multi-colored shirt. Eileen saw him and yelled, "Get out! I don't want your help. Now go back home and change that awful shirt." She knew it was impossible for a man to learn what he thinks he already knows.

Mark smiled and said, "Ha! I didn't come here to help. I only want a Guinness. Please don't disappoint me on my last day of freedom."

Eileen smiled and yelled out, "Freedom? You should thank your lucky stars there's even one woman in all of Ireland who'd have you." She handed him his pint and he walked back to a corner table so he could relax and watch all the commotion going on. Near lunch time, the first guests started arriving. By early afternoon the place was packed, and by evening it had spilled over onto the sidewalks. Old Conner was back, and Mark could swear he hadn't changed his soiled pants from last night. Jims had brought his wife, Ailen and the beautiful Gabriella were greeting everyone, and Niamh, with her parents and daughter beside her, was the main attraction. GC and Layla made an appearance but didn't stay too long . . . understandably. Then, when things were in full swing, with the music playing, and people dancing, Claire came in.

She had changed from her Amish-looking dress into a short skirt and high heels, and was wearing more makeup than a Vegas showgirl. Old Conner was flabbergasted! Nearly all the men, and all the teenagers, gawked unapologetically as Claire strode up to the bar and ordered a martini.

Eileen looked at her and said, "Martini? Girl, do you know where you are? You're in Ireland, not some New York hot spot." Claire glared back at her but kept quiet. Then, Eileen pushed a pint glass of Guinness toward her and walked away. Claire noticed all the men staring at her (and most of the women) so she only sipped her Guinness, as a Dublin socialite was supposed to do.

After several minutes of searching the crowd, she finally saw Mark back in the corner away from the throngs of people. She set her pint down and sashayed toward him. She had obviously been practicing her strut in high heels because she knew exactly which way to sway to ensure all the men would notice her. Mark saw her coming, but it was too late to hide now. All he could do was hope things didn't get too weird.

"Good evening, Mark. Very nice party, thanks for inviting me."

"You're welcome, thanks for coming, Claire. You look very nice."

Claire smiled at the compliment and said, "I know, can't you see everyone staring at me?"

Mark wanted to respond, but his inner voice said to him, *"Don't! Don't let her get to you. Just keep quiet and it'll be okay."* So, he kept his mouth shut.

She asked, "Do you remember the last time I wore this dress, Mark?" He honestly didn't understand the question, so she helped him, "It was the night of the party at Ailen's house when you danced with me and kissed me."

"Oh, no . . . please don't go there. Please, Lord, help me keep quiet." This was all Mark could think. Fortunately, old Conner came to the rescue. He had followed Claire and was now standing directly behind her, staring at her legs. Mark saw him and quickly said, "Claire, let me introduce you to my old friend, Conner."

With that, Conner took one step around and started babbling in Gaelic. He leaned in and quickly kissed her on the cheek, leaving some sort of smudge mark. Claire yelled, "Get away from me you pervert." Conner just smiled and tried to shake her hand. Mark was loving it. When Conner tried to kiss her again, she abruptly turned and walked away.

Mark reached his hand and took old Conner's wrinkled hand to shake it, and said, "Thank you, buddy, I owe you one. I think she had to go to the bathroom. Why don't you go over there and wait for her?" Old Conner smiled, revealing remnants of a recent meal wedged between his teeth, spoke some gibberish, and started for the women's restroom to wait for Claire. Mark left to find Niamh and join in the hugs and congratulations everyone was giving. After a few minutes of this, he made his way over to the bar where Eileen was working her tail off and loving every minute of it (though she would never admit it).

Mark asked, "Do you need any help? Looks like you're working awfully hard."

She stopped and stared at him, saying, "You don't get good at hard things by doing easy things, Mark. I'm fine. Just go back to your bride, I'll be fine."

"Eileen, I can find a man to come back there and help you, and maybe even take you out later." He was almost kidding with that last phrase.

She stopped and leaned in close to him and said, "Mark, men are like bank accounts: without a lot of money, they don't generate a lot of interest. Now leave me alone!"

The music played, everyone danced, and most of the food was eaten, but as hard as everyone tried, the Guinness never came close to running out. Near midnight, old Conner was asleep in a chair with drool dripping off his chin, and Claire had danced with nearly every man in the pub, except Mark. At this moment, the two fiddle players and guitar player motioned for Niamh to come up to the stage. Then, he went to the microphone and said, "For our final number, folks, our guest of honor has volunteered to sing us a song."

Niamh spoke briefly to the musicians, then she said, "Mark, my love, this song is for you, I hope you like it."

There are places I remember
All my life, though some have changed
Some forever not for better

Inception

Some have gone and some remain

All these places had their moments
With lovers and friends, I still can recall
Some are dead and some are living
In my life I've loved them all

But of all these friends and lovers
There is no one compares with you
And these memories lose their meaning
When I think of love as something new

Though I know I'll never lose affection
For people and things that went before
I know I'll often stop and think about them
In my life I love you more

Though I know I'll never lose affection
For people and things that went before
I know I'll often stop and think about them
In my life I love you more, in my life I love you more

When she finished singing, all the women were crying (except Claire) and all the men were thinking, "*I wish she was marrying me.*"

Finally, people started making their way home. All of them took home bags of food, courtesy of Ailen. Niamh and Mark had hugged everyone there at least four times—except Conner, where one hug was enough. Mark, again volunteered to help clean up the mess, but Eileen wouldn't hear of it. However, Claire did offer to help, and Eileen accepted her offer. Maybe Claire is not entirely a wicked woman after all . . . anything is possible.

SIX

SUNDAY MORNING WAS OVERCAST, with short periods of sunlight breaking through, and light periods of mist and drizzle, not unusual for Ireland. Mark rose early, got dressed, and went to the Baptist church where GC was the minister. He was so nervous that he couldn't comprehend what GC's message was about. All he could think was, *"In about four hours I'm going to be marrying the most beautiful woman in the world. The woman I've dreamed about my entire life. Can I make her happy? Please, Lord, help me."*

Niamh had too many things to take care of this morning for her to go with Mark to the church service. Making sure her hair was properly done for the ceremony, although it was perfect without having anything done to it. Ensuring her makeup was just right: not too much and not too little, although she never actually needed any makeup. Trying on her wedding dress for the hundredth time . . . just to make sure it fit (it was perfect). Talking to Claire and Eileen to make sure everything was ready for the reception (with Eileen and Claire, of course it was). And, dressing her daughter, Ennis, who was so excited she couldn't be still (just like her mother).

When the church service ended, someone had to tap Mark's shoulder to let him know it was time to leave. GC assured him everything would be fine. Layla walked him out and hugged his neck, telling him everything would be fine. He took a deep breath and said, "Thanks, Susan, I appreciate that." Layla had no idea who "Susan" was, but she understood how nervous the groom could be. Mark tried to check in on Claire to see if everything was on schedule—she wouldn't let him in the restaurant. Then he tried to check in on Eileen—she wouldn't let him in either. He didn't know what to do for the next three hours. He only knew he couldn't sit down and wait; he had to do something.

He hopped in his car and drove over to Burtonport to see his friend Jims at his pub. When he arrived, Jims was already dressed for the wedding and was talking to his bartender about some business. He was surprised to see Mark; after all, the wedding was only a couple of hours away. He tried to have Mark sit at the bar, but Mark was too nervous. He tried to get him to sit at a table in the corner—no luck there either. Finally, he said, "Hop in the car, let's ride up to the cliff." That sounded great.

Jims drove up the winding road and parked about fifteen feet away from the cliff's edge. The wind, as usual, was whipping pretty good, so they didn't get out. They sat in silence for a few minutes, feeling the wind rock the car gently as it finished its journey over the ocean, all the way from America, with no obstacle to hinder it until now. Mark replayed all the times he sat up here by himself yearning for Niamh. He remembered the first time he kissed her; the first time he held her hand; the many times he dreamed of her, whispering to her in his mind. Jims could tell Mark's mind was reliving all these memories, so he never said a word—which is a hard thing to do for an Irishman. After about forty-five minutes, without a word being spoken, Jims drove them back into town. They both got out of the car and Mark hugged him. Neither man said another word as Mark got into his own car and drove back to Dungloe in anticipation of the happiest day of his life.

* * *

Mark somehow got dressed and made his way to the church nearly two hours before the 3:00 wedding. He stood inside the front door to greet people as they arrived. He wasn't supposed to do that, but he couldn't help it. No one except GC and Layla arrived for over an hour. GC walked up to Mark and said, "Everything you can imagine is almost real. Just have faith, my friend."

Mark took a deep breath and replied, "I have faith, GC; I just need some proof to back it up." When GC went to his office, Mark visited the bathroom again, for the umpteenth time this afternoon. More people were arriving and when he returned, he saw a regular customer from the pub come in with a new girlfriend that Mark didn't recognize. The girlfriend went in ahead to find a seat and Mark looked at his friend and said, "Hey, Seamus, she's a pretty girl."

Seamus leaned in close and replied, "Every girl is beautiful. Sometimes it takes the right amount of alcohol to see it." He winked at Mark, who smartly didn't reply.

Jims arrived with his wife, who was already crying. Old Conner was following a few steps behind them and had changed his old, soiled pants and had attempted to shave—without much success. Soon, the church was filling up. Niamh was in the back with her bridesmaids, just as nervous as Mark. Her mother was fighting back tears and her Pa was telling everyone off-color jokes. Then, Claire arrived.

She was dressed appropriately and looked very nice. As she walked up the front steps, she noticed Mark and motioned for him to come outside to see her. He did. He didn't want to, but he did. She hugged him and kissed him on the cheek, then shook his hand. When she pulled her hand away, Mark felt something in his hand. It was a piece of paper folded tightly in a square. Before he could unfold it, Claire said, "I'm very happy for you, Mark. But . . . if for some reason, things don't work out, that is my new phone number. Call me anytime."

"What? Claire, are you stupid?" He took the piece of paper and threw it on the floor. Claire turned and walked into the church. Mark was fuming and needed to clam down quickly. He walked out front, down the steps, only to take a few deep breaths.

When he came back into the church, Eileen was waiting on him, grabbed his arm, and said, "Come with me." She pulled him over to a corner and said, "Did you just call Claire stupid? She's in the church crying."

Mark was stunned. He looked back at Eileen and replied, "I would never call Claire stupid. I only "asked" her if she was stupid." Eileen was thoroughly confused. Mark continued, "She tried to give me her phone number in case things didn't work out with me and Niamh."

When Eileen heard this, her face turned red and she said, "I'll take care of this. I'm sorry, Mark." She turned and marched back into the church. Mark decided one more, quick trip into the restroom was in order. When he came out, he was summoned up to the front of the church—it was time.

Mark stood up front with his best man, Ailen. When Niamh appeared at the back of the church, and Mark saw her, his entire coherency was obliterated. His mind went blank. He totally forgot about Claire. He had no thoughts at all except of Niamh. If there is such a thing as an "out-of-body experience," this was it. As she started her walk down the aisle with her father, Mark slowly regained consciousness and viability. He didn't notice anyone else in the church; he never saw Niamh's father next to her. He forgot Ailen was next to him and almost forgot why he was there—the only thing he saw and thought of was Niamh.

Her veil was down, but Mark could see those eyes . . . oh, those eyes that had mesmerized him since that first day on the cliff. Her face, her smile, her light brown hair tinted with red—everything about her was perfect. Everything about her was his dream come true. He hoped he could speak during the ceremony; at this point, he wasn't sure of that.

Niamh was nearly the opposite of Mark in her emotions and reactions. She knew how special this was. She knew she had the man of her dreams. She knew there was no one on earth who could be as happy as she was. It was as if Venus and Mars had finally aligned, and the cosmos was in perfect union. There was no way her life could be any better.

GC arranged everyone in their proper positions and began the ceremony. Mark and Niamh were facing each other, holding hands, as GC spoke. Niamh heard every word. Mark heard nothing. The only thing he could see or hear was her. Nothing else. When GC asked him if he would take this woman to be his wedded wife, he didn't answer. Only because he didn't hear anything. After a few seconds of silence, Niamh squeezed his hand and GC said, "Mark?" Only then did he come back to reality. GC continued the service, and it was a dream come true for all those involved. Until . . .

Near the end of the ceremony, when GC asked, "If anyone here has any objections to this marriage, let him speak now, or forever, hereafter hold his peace."

"I object!" Everyone in the church turned towards the rear where the voice had come from. A middle-aged man, in a suit, stood up and said again, "I object. This man cannot marry this woman today."

Everyone was completely stunned. GC asked, "What are you talking about, sir? What is your objection?"

The man spoke louder and said, "I have come to arrest this man and take him back to North Carolina for theft and fraud." As he said this, two uniformed officers walked into the church and started down the aisle toward Mark. The man followed the officers and stopped directly in front of Mark, who was still holding Niamh's hand. "I'm sorry for the timing, but I just confirmed your identity, and I cannot allow this ceremony to progress."

Mark was so stunned he could not speak. Niamh stared at the man and said, "What are you talking about? Why are you doing this?"

"Ma'am, I'm sorry. This man, Paul Alfred, or Mark McCarty as he's known now, is being arrested for fraud and attempted theft of a million-dollar life insurance policy. I have no alternative but to take him into custody and let the courts sort all this out. I'm sorry." As he finished, the uniformed officers handcuffed Mark and started walking him out of the church. Mark still hadn't spoken. Niamh ran after them and grabbed Mark, but the officers pulled her away. Mark could not speak, all he could do was stare back at Niamh and see the tears coming out of those beautiful, emerald, green eyes.

Ailen tried to stop the policemen, but there was nothing he could do. He assured Mark he would take care of everything and not to worry. An easy thing to say but very hard to do, especially when you've just been torn from the most important person in your life.

SEVEN

MARK WAS TAKEN TO THE AIRPORT and booked on the first flight available to Charlotte, North Carolina. At least they'd taken off the handcuffs for the flight back to America. Ailen assured Niamh he would take care of everything. He then went to his office and called his lawyer who told him he'd check into things and call him back shortly. That was an understatement—he called back in less than thirty minutes. According to the lawyer, Mark was arrested because there was a million-dollar life insurance policy on him that had been cashed when he obviously wasn't dead.

Mark's ex-wife apparently had assumed he was dead after he changed his name and moved to Ireland. She did hire a Private Investigator to look for him, but Mark had covered his tracks well. After a year with no word, the courts declared Mark legally dead, and his ex-wife cashed in the policy. Mark was completely unaware of any of these circumstances; however, insurance companies don't just give up a million dollars without checking. It took them a while, but eventually they realized Paul Alfred had changed his name to Mark McCarty and was living in Ireland. They assumed that he and his ex-wife were in collusion to collect the money. His ex-wife had dumped her snake-of-a-lawyer boyfriend when she collected her million dollars, and he didn't like it. He let the insurance company know that he thought there was a scam going on. That's all it took.

Ailen started collecting all the facts. He had the documents where Mark had legally changed his name, and he also had Mark's bank statements which showed had did not have anything close to a million dollars. He had his lawyer call a reputable firm in Winston-Salem to take over the case. This firm, Anderson & Christopher, was ready when Mark's plane landed. They immediately got him released on bail, paid for by Ailen, and then worked on trying to get the trial moved up as fast as possible. The only thing they couldn't do was revoke the order that Mark could not leave the state until the trial. He had to stay in Winston-Salem until he was proven innocent.

Ailen made a reservation for Mark at the Kimpton Cardinal Hotel in downtown Winston-Salem, which was the original home of RJR Tobacco Company. Winston was Mark's home, so he knew this building very well. After checking in, the first thing he did was call Niamh. She was, understandably, very upset; yet, she wasn't too emotional, given the circumstances. Ailen had also assured her that he would take care of everything, and that Mark would be home soon. And Ailen didn't lie about anything.

Ailen, and the beautiful Gabriella, packed their bags and made the next available flight to North Carolina as well. Their path led them to Raleigh, instead of Charlotte, which was much better than fighting all the traffic Charlotte had to offer. When they finally arrived in Winston, Mark was waiting on them in the side bar at the hotel, sipping a hot cup of coffee. Gabriella ran to him and hugged him tightly, assuring him that Ailen would handle everything. Mark said, "I know . . . I know."

"I mean EVERYTHING, Mark! Don't worry about Niamh, this court thing, the costs—NOTHING!"

She was still hugging him as Ailen was smiling at the scene, and everyone else in the bar was staring at this unusual happening. When the beautiful Gabriella finally turned Mark loose, not that he didn't enjoy the embrace, Ailen and he bumped fists, then did a short manly nod of the head, as true Irishmen should. Mark then said, "Let's go to Finnegan's Wake for dinner; I'd really like to see Opie again."

Ailen sadly told him that Finnegan's had closed. It was Mark's favorite restaurant in town. "Closed? What happened?"

"Couldn't keep staff during the pandemic. But I think Opie fell in love with a young lady, at least I think she's young, so he's doing okay. And, you never know what might happen in the future." As he finished saying this, Ailen's local detective friend, Desmond, walked in the bar. Mark knew Desmond from when he had visited Ireland previously. Ailen had hired Desmond to look into all the charges surrounding Mark and the ex-wife to see what he could find. And Desmond was good at finding all the dirt under everyone's fingernails. Also, Desmond's wife, Stella, and Gabriella were sisters—it was not only a working trip but a family reunion as well.

Over dinner at Ryan's, one of Winston-Salem's finest restaurants, Desmond told them that he'd already learned that Mark's ex-wife had indeed cashed in the million-dollar life insurance policy, then sold her house, and moved to Holden Beach, where she bought a condo on the coast. From what Desmond could learn, she was quickly burning up the money while searching for a rich husband. After that information, they dropped all the serious talk and then listened to Desmond tell story after story of things happening in Winston and his life. Mark loved hearing it all . . . Winston still meant a lot to him.

* * *

After the wedding fiasco, Niamh, her daughter, and her parents all went to the house Niamh and Mark were going to live in on the coast near Ailen's house. Niamh's mother made tea, her daughter, Ennis, started playing video games, and her dad took a nap. Niamh sat by the window staring out into the bay at several small islands. Her mother handed her the cup of tea and wisely left her daughter alone. Niamh sipped the tea slowly, as good Irish girls do, and stared blankly out to sea, thinking of Mark, alone in America, not knowing what was going to happen. Then her phone rang.

"Hello."

"Niamh, it's Mark. Don't worry, everything is going to be fine. Ailen is handling things and, hopefully, I'll be back soon. You know I love you more than anything in the world, right?"

"I know, Mark, it's just . . . why did this have to happen on the happiest day of our lives?"

"I don't know, honey; but it did. As soon as I get back, we'll do it all over again—better than before."

Niamh didn't reply for a moment, then answered, "Mark, I think I'd just like to elope. Maybe drive to Galway, or Killarney, someplace fun, and just do it quickly—me and you. What do you think? My mom could keep Ennis for a few days, and we could be alone."

If Niamh wanted to elope, they'd elope. If she wanted to move to Tanzania, they'd move to Tanzania. If she wanted to hike across the South Pole, they'd hike . . . Mark would do anything she wanted. She was his life. Without her, there would be no life. "Sounds great to me," he replied. "Pick out anywhere you want, and we'll go." They talked for twenty more minutes, nothing of relevance, just having that connection was enough. Strangely enough, that phone call settled them both down and they each slept calmly through the night.

The next day, Desmond, Ailen, and his lawyers spent the day at the courthouse, producing documents, filing requisitions, and fighting the endless array of red tape this entire fiasco had produced. Eventually, a judge told them he'd review everything and let them know in the morning what the next step would be. One of the lawyers, Mr. Christopher, tried to assure everyone that everything looked good, not to worry. The other lawyer, Mr.

Anderson, was extremely nervous, but confident as well. He told everyone to go home; he would contact the judge, after hours, and try to get his feelings on the case. Apparently, the two were old college dormmates at UNC-Chapel Hill. In reality, the judge's wife, Dail, and Mr. Anderson's wife, Shirley, were first cousins, and their families were very close.

Ailen had made reservations for everyone at the Katherine, an elegant restaurant at the hotel where Mark was staying. Desmond and Stella, Ailen and the beautiful Gabriella, and the lonely Mark all enjoyed a fabulous meal. Desmond and Stella ate off each other's plates and sipped each other's wine while playing footsie with each other. Ailen and Gabriella kept staring into each other's eyes and hearts—their love obvious for everyone in the restaurant to see. And Mark . . . well, he wanted to start crying so badly he could hardly eat. So, instead of eating . . . he drank. And drank. And drank.

Finally, Ailen noticed his friend was on the verge of either passing out or displaying his redneck roots and fighting someone . . . anyone; at this point in time, Mark did not care who. Ailen said, "Hey, buddy, I think it's about time I got you back to your room."

"Huh?" Mark replied, "What do you mean?"

Ailen answered, "I mean, I think it's time for you to go to bed."

Mark suddenly stood up, knocking a glass onto the floor, and stammered, "I'm not as think as you drunk I am!" And with that eloquent statement, he bent over and threw up on the table. Fortunately, everyone except Desmond was spared the repercussions of the vomit splatter. Before Mark could fall completely to the floor, Ailen caught him and settled him back into the chair. The girls were trying not to giggle too much, while Desmond was sloshing water on his shirt and pants, trying to get the vomit stains out.

Between them, Desmond and Ailen got him to his room and took his shoes off before laying him on the bed. Ailen wrote a note that said, "Call me, Ailen" and put it on a table next to the phone. They waited until he started snoring before they called the girls, telling them to take the car and go on home. They decided to stay in the room for a while to make sure Mark was okay and stayed asleep. After about two hours they felt it was safe enough to leave.

Mark woke at about 6:00 AM to go to the bathroom and saw the note next to the phone as he returned. He picked it up and read it, "*Call me, Ailen,*" and thought, "*Why would I call myself Ailen?*" Before he could formulate an answer, he took his trousers off, then his shirt, laid back down, and was sound asleep in less than a minute.

At some point that morning, Mark woke and heard his cell phone ringing and someone knocking on the door at the same time. He couldn't figure out which to answer first, the phone or the door; then he realized he had no pants on, so he answered his phone first. "Hello."

"Mark, open the door." It was Ailen and he didn't sound particularly happy. Mark looked out the peep hole and saw Ailen by himself, so he opened the door, still wearing only his boxers. Ailen looked at him, closed the door, and walked in.

Before he could say anything, Mark said, "I'm sorry. I don't know what happened. I feel terrible . . . literally, I feel terrible."

Ailen had brought some Extra Strength Tylenol with him and handed them to Mark, then he said, "At some point, we've all parked in the wrong garage." Mark took three of the pills before Ailen told him to hop in the shower and get dressed; they had a meeting with the lawyers in about an hour. That statement did more than anything to sober Mark up very quickly.

EIGHT

THE NEXT MORNING, Niamh woke early but didn't get up. She stayed in bed and allowed her mind to race, while her mother prepared breakfast for everyone. She wasn't upset . . . it was more that she just needed some time alone. To think. To reflect. To dream. To hope.

It was during this time that her phone rang. She was hoping it was Mark calling again, but with the time difference, it was much too early for a call from America. The call was from Layla, the preacher GC's wife, and a good friend of Niamh's. She wanted to assure her they were thinking of her and wanted to comfort her in any way they could. Niamh appreciated the call, but melancholy and self-pity were trying to invade her consciousness. She told Layla, "I feel as though God has forgotten about me. How could He let this happen? I don't understand."

Layla understood. She knew how her friend was feeling and she wanted to reassure her that God had not forgotten about her. She said, "Niamh, have you ever considered that God has fallen in love with you? Look, He sends you flowers every spring. He sends you sunshine every morning. Whenever you want to talk, He listens to you. He can live anywhere in the universe, but He chose you, your heart. God didn't promise days without pain, laughter without sorrow, or sun without rain; but He did promise strength for the day, comfort for the tears, and light for the way. He chose you, Niamh. And He also chose Mark for you."

"I know, Layla. Thank you so much . . . I needed to hear that. It's just that things are so difficult now."

"Niamh, real difficulties can be overcome; it is only the imaginary ones that are unconquerable. Look, I'm here anytime you need to talk, or if you just need me. Anytime, anywhere, simply let me know."

Niamh needed that. The short conversation renewed her, invigorated her, and enabled her to get out of bed and start the process of living again and looking forward to the future. She went into the living room and her mother brought her a cup of tea. As she was sipping the tea, staring out the window, her phone rang again. This time it was Claire.

"Niamh, how are you? Is there anything I can do? Do you want me to bring you lunch? Do you . . ."

"Claire! Hold on; I'm fine. You don't need to do anything . . . I'm fine. Everything will get worked out, please don't worry about me." Even though Claire had always been a thorn in Mark's side, Niamh liked her and in her own way, felt a little sorry for her about the way things ended with Claire's own marriage. "Mark and Ailen are in the States, and they'll sort this entire mess out and we'll set a new date for the wedding; it'll all work out. Don't worry. How are you doing? I hear things are well in the restaurant."

Claire liked hearing that and almost started crying . . . no one ever gave her compliments; she wasn't used to it. She said, "Thanks Niamh, it's been a little hard for me since I returned. It's hard to forget the past."

"I can't imagine what you've gone through. I'm so happy you're okay."

Claire took a deep breath and replied, "I'm not sure where I'd be now if Mark hadn't called me. I just don't know."

"Even if Mark hadn't called, this is your home, Claire, you belong here. Where else would you go?"

Claire took a moment, then answered, "I don't know, Niamh. At that time in my life, I just wanted to go . . . " She paused briefly, then continued, "I wanted to go to the least inhabited; least inhibited; least civilized; least governed; least priest-ridden; most arid; most hostile; most lonesome; most grim, bleak, barren, desolate, and savage quarter in all of Ireland—the best part by far. So far. Where? I'll never tell."

When she finished her thought, both women were quiet. Both women understood. Neither woman needed to, or could, say anything more.

* * *

Ailen had set up a meeting with the lawyers that morning at 10:00 in downtown Winston-Salem. Mark got dressed as Ailen and Desmond waited downstairs for him. When he got off the elevator, Ailen looked at him and said, "My God, man, look at you!"

Mark stopped and said, "What?"

Ailen was flabbergasted and replied, "What? Look at you! We're going to meet the solicitors and you're wearing blue jeans and a t-shirt!"

"Ailen," Mark tried to say in a soothing tone, "this is America, not Ireland. People here don't dress in suits and ties like you guys do in Ireland. We stopped doing that twenty years ago. I'm fine; you, however, are grossly overdressed." Ailen had on one of his tailor-made suits and looked fantastic. Desmond had on a faded blue coat, with a half-tied knot of a tie, and khakis, with loafers. Mark continued, "We're all fine, let's go."

They arrived early at the lawyer's offices because, well, Ailen was always early. Never late. A very attractive secretary offered them coffee, which Desmond and Mark accepted. Ailen asked, "Do you have tea?"

The secretary, who had an oddly spelled name, Rhyanne, answered, "Yes, of course. Sweet or unsweet?"

Before Ailen could figure out what she meant, Desmond said, "No, he's fine. Thank you." Just then, one of the lawyers, Mr. Anderson, opened a door and invited them all into his office. He was dressed immaculately in a light blue suit as he showed them in. His partner, Mr. Christopher, also had on a light blue suit, just a tad darker than his partner's, but very close. After handshakes and small talk, they got right down to business.

Mr. Anderson said, "Thanks for joining our team. We've been studying your documents and all the associated information we've discovered. I don't think there are going to be any problems or issues, other than it might take some time for the courts to validate everything and set things straight." Everyone smiled at that statement, especially Mark.

Then, Mr. Christopher added, "As you know, the court has ordered Mr. McCarty here not to leave the state until everything is finalized. We have a fund available here at our firm to help with necessary expenses, such as clothing, while he's here in North Carolina." At that point everyone turned to look at Mark, the only person in the room not in a coat and tie.

Ailen stared directly into Mark's eyes as he answered, "That won't be necessary, gentlemen; I'll make sure Mr. McCarty is properly dressed in the future." Mark started to say something, but Ailen stood and said forcefully, "Properly dressed!" Mark, wisely, kept his mouth shut.

It was good that the lawyers assured them everything would be okay. It was disappointing to learn it would not be a speedy resolution. Mark was going to be in Winston-Salem until the courts ruled. They left the lawyers' offices and walked down the street a couple of blocks to a coffee shop. Ailen said, "Wait here, I'll be right back." They waited. He came back out and said, "Let's go." He started walking faster and they tried their best to follow him. At the next corner he walked into another place called Camino's. They waited and about ten seconds later Ailen opened the door and said, "C'mon in. They have tea here . . . real tea!"

Ailen took his tea outside to a table on the street. Mark ordered more coffee to aid in his hangover recuperation, and Desmond ordered a Dr. Pepper. They sat in silence and watched the motor traffic and the pedestrian traffic pass by as they all sipped their drinks. Finally, Ailen said, "You can stay at Gabriella's place until this thing is sorted out. Desmond, you take care of everything and make sure nothing goes wrong. I'm leaving for Ireland tonight. Any questions?" Both men knew better than to ask any questions. They both nodded and continued to sip their drinks.

Ailen's wife, the beautiful Gabriella, was from Winston-Salem and had kept her residence after the marriage. She and Ailen used it on their trips back to visit. Mark knew where it was, but unfortunately, he also knew where his heart was . . . and it wasn't at Gabriella's home in the West End section of Winston-Salem.

Ailen left them after he finished his tea, so he could pack for his flight back to Ireland. Desmond returned to his office, and Mark waited for him to leave before he grabbed his phone and called Niamh. Just the sound of her voice calmed him immensely and almost made his head stop hurting. He explained everything that happened and all the consequences as well. She knew he would have to stay there a while, but it was still hard. They talked until Mark's phone started beeping with a low battery. They talked about nothing, and they talked about everything. They didn't want to stop but Mark didn't have his phone plug with him. He promised to call later. She promised everything would be okay. He had been believing her for over three hundred years now; no reason she would lie to him now.

NINE

MARK CHECKED OUT OF THE HOTEL and took a cab over to a rental car company where he picked out a Jeep Patriot for the stay in his old hometown. He then drove to Gabriella's home in the West End section of Winston-Salem. He didn't even unpack his suitcase, he just dropped it off and drove downtown to visit his favorite restaurant in Winston, Finnegan's Wake. If his personal life wasn't bad enough, seeing the sign on the front door that read "CLOSED" only magnified his depression. He stood in front of the door and stared at the sign. He couldn't understand how or why this could have happened. Finnegan's was his favorite restaurant, the best place, his personal resort to get away. He kept staring at the "CLOSED" sign, hoping it would magically change. The ingenuity of self-deception is inexhaustible.

That experience extinguished his hunger thoughts. He decided to walk down the street to Desmond's office, just because he had nowhere else to go. Desmond's business was only two blocks away and up a flight of stairs. When Mark walked up the last step, he heard giggling and rustling noises inside Desmond's office. He leaned in close to the door and was certain he heard Desmond's voice, so he knocked on the door. Desmond yelled out, "Who is it?"

"It's Mark, can I come in?" Then he heard more rustling and noises before Desmond came to unlock the door. When he opened the door, his tie was loose and crooked, his hair was a mess, and he didn't have any shoes on. Mark said, "Are you okay?"

"Yeah, yeah, I'm just . . . finishing up some work. What's wrong?"

"Nothing's wrong, I just thought I'd come over and see you. I went to Finnegan's and saw it was closed. What happened?"

Before Desmond could answer, his wife, Stella, came from the back office and said, "Hi, Mark, good to see you." Her lipstick was slightly smeared around her cheeks and Mark suddenly realized he'd interrupted a tete-a-tete between the newly married couple. Before he could say anything, Stella continued, "Well, I'll see you two later." She gave Mark a quick hug and scrambled out the door.

Mark looked over at Desmond and said, "I'm so sorry."

"No problem, I'll take care of that unfinished business when she comes back after lunch . . . if you know what I mean." Mark didn't want to know what he meant. Desmond quickly changed the subject and said, "Let's go. I want to show you how Winston has changed since you moved away." Desmond had a seven-year-old Mercedes that was in dire need of a cleaning, but it ran well, and he drove Mark all around town. They visited Mark's old house, some new businesses, and the Innovation Quarter, where most of Winston's new growth and development was taking place.

Desmond thought Mark might be getting a little homesick since he didn't speak, but that was not the case. Mark's silence was not because of homesickness, but rather lovesickness . . . his only thoughts were of Niamh. Fortunately for Mark, Desmond's cell phone rang, and he was needed at work. Mark hopped out downtown near Camino's and walked the streets of Winston as his mind wandered to the green hills and valleys, the mountains and coasts, and the green-eyed beauty that was and is Ireland.

* * *

Ailen caught a direct flight from Raleigh to Shannon, Ireland. He had to get back, plus he was paying Desmond very well to take care of Mark. After he finally got back home to Dungloe and spent the evening with his wife, he went into town the following day to update everyone on what was happening. He first went to Niamh's house and reassured her everything was okay, and when Ailen tells you everything will be fine—it will!

Next, he went into town to check on the pub, the restaurant, and all the other businesses he owned. Since Mark ran everything for him, Ailen didn't really know what he was looking at, but he tried. In the pub, he ordered a Guinness from Eileen and then listened to her tell him everything he SHOULD be doing to ensure Mark's safe return. All he had to do was keep nodding and keep sipping . . . Eileen had the answer for everything.

His next stop was the restaurant, where he walked in with the intention of sitting at a table for lunch when Claire stopped him and asked, "Do you have a reservation?"

"No. Do I need one, Claire? I do own this place, you know."

He was sure this comment would elicit an apology from Claire. He was wrong. "It doesn't matter who you are, Ailen. If you want this place run like it should be run, then you'll follow the rules like everyone else. Am I right?"

Ailen thought a moment, started to fire her, then relented, and said, "Okay, you're right. Can I get a reservation please?" Which seemed like an odd question to ask since the place was barely half full.

Claire answered, "No, sir, I'm sorry; we're expecting a full house very soon. Call me back in about an hour." Then she turned and walked away. The cashier and all the other staff immediately disappeared in the back out of fear. The few customers sitting there were waiting for Ailen to explode and fire everyone . . . but he didn't. He left. He wasn't happy, but he left. He'd known Claire a long time and he knew when to pick his battles. This wasn't the time.

Mark ended up back at the hotel and called Niamh again, just because he could, and because he wanted to, and because he needed to. The call soothed them both and reassured them both that everything would be fine. After the call, he decided to walk the streets again in order to calm his nerves and pass the time. Desmond had invited him over to his house for dinner, but after his "interruption" earlier in the day, he decided to let them have their privacy tonight. He walked for over an hour until he noticed a food truck in front of a local brewery named Fiddlin' Fish. He ordered a burger and fries and went in the brewery to have a drink and wait for his food. He ordered an Ardmore Amber, lighter than a Guinness but better than a Yuengling. The brewery was not busy when the lady bartender brought him his drink, so she asked Mark, "Haven't seen you around before. Are you new here?"

Mark answered, "Not really . . . I grew up here but moved away for a while. I'm just visiting now."

"A woman?" The bartender asked.

"Huh?"

"Are you visiting a woman? That's what usually brings men around."

"Oh, no, I'm not. Just a little business I have to take care of. Then I'll be going back home."

The bartender, named Billie, asked, "Where's home?"

"Ireland."

Billie seemed shocked and asked, "Ireland?"

"Yeah, Ireland."

"I ain't never met anyone from Ireland. It is indeed an honor, sir." She stuck her hand out and said, "I'm Billie. Nice to meet you."

Mark shook her hand and said, "Mark. Good to meet you too, Billie."

Billie smiled and asked, "Are you married, Mark?"

"I was married to a girl from Winston-Salem at one time, but not any longer. She wasn't happy, so we got a divorce."

Billie nodded, then added, "Well, how can a woman be expected to be happy with a man who insists on treating her as if she were a perfectly normal human being?"

Mark figured he'd better not comment further on this subject, so he asked, "How about you, Billie? Are you married?"

"Been married twice, Mark, and I've had bad luck with both of my husbands. The first one left me and the second one didn't." And fortunately for Mark, his hamburger arrived just in time. Billie continued, "I'll let you eat your dinner. Good to meet you, Mark. Cheerio!" Mark didn't want to tell Billie that "Cheerio" wasn't an Irish idiom, so he enjoyed his burger and fries and even had a second Ardmore Amber as his mind thought of nothing but emerald eyes and rolling green hills. Few people have the imagination for reality . . . Mark did.

* * *

Mark spent two more days in Winston-Salem as he waited for Desmond and the lawyers to sort out everything. The third morning, Desmond received a call from one of the lawyers who told him that the judge was willing to work out a plea deal and avoid a trial if this was acceptable to Mark. Mark's first question was "How much?" What Mark didn't know was that Desmond had first called Ailen, in Ireland, and presented the plea deal to him. Ailen immediately accepted it. It seemed high to him, but he knew how the courts and lawyers worked. He just wanted the entire affair to end. He told Desmond to tell Mark that the plea deal would cost him only a couple of thousand dollars and no jail time. True, there was no jail time, however, the fine was much higher than a couple of thousand dollars. Ailen knew Mark couldn't afford it, so he paid it and told Desmond to not say a word.

Mark suspected something was up; Desmond was a little too edgy and non-committal, but if this would get him back home, then GREAT! They went by the lawyer's offices, signed the documents, and handed them a certified check. Mark then went back to the hotel, called the airlines, made his reservation, and started packing. Desmond drove him to Greensboro to catch a flight to Atlanta, then on to Dublin. Nothing going into the Shannon airport was available, but that didn't matter. He just wanted to be moving.

TEN

FINALLY, MARK WAS SEATED ON THE FLIGHT BACK to Dublin. An older man, dressed in a coat and tie was seated next to him. As soon as Mark fastened his seat belt the man introduced himself, "Hello, my name's Conrad. Looks like it's going to be a packed flight, doesn't it?"

Mark didn't really want to speak with anyone. He only wanted to doze and think of Niamh, but he answered, "Yes sir, it does."

The older man nodded, then asked, "So, you're going to Dublin, huh?"

If it had been a younger man, Mark would've given a smart-aleck answer, but this gentleman seemed kind and a little lonely, so Mark dutifully answered, "Yes sir, I'm going to Dublin."

"Do you live there?"

"No sir, I live up on the northwest coast in a little town called Dungloe."

The older man smiled and said, "Aye, I've been to Dungloe, I used to pass through it on business years ago. It's a nice little village." At this time, the plane started taxiing down the runway and Conrad stared out the window. Mark noticed he had a rather old, worn, wedding ring which he kept spinning around his finger. As they sped down the runway for liftoff, the man stopped spinning his ring and grabbed the armrest tightly instead.

After the plane had leveled off a bit, Mark thought he should say something to reassure the older man that everything was okay, "You know these planes are marvels of engineering. They fly so easily . . . it's amazing how safe they are."

The man then started spinning his ring again and answered, "Let's hope so. You know, aerodynamically, the bumble bee shouldn't be able to fly at all, but it doesn't know that, so it goes on flying anyway. Let's hope our pilots are like that. I truly don't understand how it all works, Mark, but I've learned that when you expect things to happen, strangely enough, they do."

Mark nodded, then turned to look around at one of the flight attendants passing by, a young lady with a nice smile. Conrad asked, "She's pretty, isn't she?"

"Yes sir. She is."

"Are you married?"

"No sir, but I am engaged and hope to be married very soon."

"Well, congratulations! Tell me about her." That's all it took. Mark then started and proceeded to tell Conrad all about Niamh. Her green eyes, and hair tinted so slightly with red, her smile, her laugh, her interests, her daughter, and the long road it took for them to find each other. Conrad sat and smiled and seemed enthralled with the story of Niamh.

When Mark paused, he thought a bit, then said, "I guess it's quite an impossibility that we ever met each other. I'm not sure how to explain it to people."

Conrad patted his arm and replied, "Impossible is just an opinion. Don't try to figure out what other people want to hear from you; just figure out what you have to say." And so, he did. Mark spent the next four hours telling Conrad about Niamh, about his life, about the struggle to find her, and about adjusting to life in Ireland. He even told him about his ex-wife and the insurance scam. Conrad was the best listener Mark had ever met. He never interrupted and only asked a few questions. Whenever Mark would look directly at him, Conrad would only nod a little and smile.

When Mark had run out of things to say about his love life, Conrad asked, "You say you were raised in North Carolina, Mark?"

"Yes, sir, I sure was."

"Well, I love the old TV program, *The Andy Griffith Show*. That was set in North Carolina, wasn't it?"

Mark proudly beamed, "Yes sir. It was. I still love that show. Mayberry certainly was a peaceful little town."

Conrad then said, "Well, you know the reason why Mayberry was so peaceful and quiet don't you?" Before Mark could answer, he continued, "Because nobody was married! Andy, Aunt Bee, Barney, Floyd, Howard, Goober, Gomer, Sam, Earnest T. Bass, Helen, Thelma Lou, Clara, and, of course, Opie were all single. The only married person was Otis and he stayed drunk."

Before Mark could comprehend that statement, or respond, the flight attendants started preparing everyone for landing. As the plane pulled up to the terminal, all the passengers started getting up and retrieving their luggage from the overhead bins. Mark was seated on the aisle, so he got up quickly and had to move forward a bit to reach his luggage. As he did, other passengers from across the aisle also rose and stepped out to get their luggage. Conrad stayed seated while all this fuss was happening. Mark looked at him, but Conrad was busy twirling his ring and looking out the window.

Mark figured he would wait just inside the terminal and say his goodbyes to Conrad and maybe even get his cellphone number. Once inside, he stood over to the side and waited, and waited, and waited. Conrad never came out. As the flight attendants started coming out, Mark stopped one of them and told them about Conrad, that he hadn't come out of the plane. This young woman set her luggage down and went back into the airplane to see if Conrad needed any help. She searched the entire plane and the restrooms—no Conrad. The airplane was completely empty.

She came back out and told Mark the plane was empty. He didn't know what to say, except, "Are you sure?"

"Yes sir. Quite sure. There's no one on the plane."

Mark then looked all around the terminal—nothing. He went to the counter and asked for help in finding Conrad. They asked for his last name—Mark didn't know his last name . . . he never asked. They couldn't page Conrad or offer any other help. Mark stood to the side and continued to stare around the terminal. Nothing. He finally started his slow walk to the luggage carousel staring at every older person in the concourse. He never saw Conrad and couldn't understand why.

He made his way to the train station nearby and took the train to Galway where he would switch again for a smaller train into Dungloe. He knew he could've called Ailen and he would have sent someone to come and pick him up, but he liked the train. He enjoyed the scenery on the way through the countryside. So many shades of green, the small lakes and streams, the fields, and all the little things that make Ireland so appealing. On the train, he called Niamh and they spoke for nearly an hour; neither of them wanting to hang up. She finally had to leave to take care of her daughter but promised to call him back later.

Mark changed trains and sat by the window on his trip to Dungloe. He thought about the old man, Conrad. They passed a small lake and he saw a man on the shoreline holding a fishing rod, not moving. He thought to himself, *"There's a fine line between fishing and just standing on the shore looking like an idiot."* The next thing he knew, someone was shaking his shoulder telling him this was his stop. He had fallen asleep and drooled down his chin. He didn't care. He was just happy to be home.

The train station was near the town center, so he walked into town and went into the restaurant to tell Claire he was back. She saw him enter and walked up to him saying, "Where have you been while we've all been working so hard?" Before he could answer, she walked away. She hadn't changed. At least she knew he was back. Then he walked down the street to the bar where he met Eileen sitting outside on a bench. She said, "Hope the trip was good. Is everything settled with the courts?"

"Yeah, everything is fine. We'll be setting a new wedding date soon. Is everything okay here?"

"Why wouldn't it be? Don't you trust me, Mark?" Before he could answer, her cell phone rang. She looked at it and said, "I need to take this. Good to have you back. Hope the train ride was good." Then she turned and went inside to answer her cell phone.

Mark thought, *"How did she know I took the train? I didn't tell her anything about a train ride. How did she know that?"* But that was Eileen. She always seemed to know things unexplainably. He made his way home to shower, change clothes, and go over to Niamh's house. He couldn't wait to get there. Niamh knew Mark was coming over, so she arranged for her parents to take her daughter out for a lengthy dinner. That would give them chance to be alone and discuss the past, the present, and the future, among other things.

Mark knocked on her door and she immediately flew into his arms. There would be no discussing any items for quite some time. Eventually, he explained everything that happened in North Carolina, and she filled him in on all the gossip and news of Dungloe. Then, as they steered the conversation toward their impending wedding, there was a knock on the door. Niamh knew her parents wouldn't be back for at least another hour. She had no idea who it could be. She rose and went to open the door. Mark sat and watched. Niamh opened the door and screamed, then collapsed on the floor, unconscious.

ELEVEN

MARK RAN TO HER AND CRADLED HER HEAD, saying, "Niamh, Niamh . . . can you hear me?" Then he noticed movement in the doorway and looked up to see a man standing there carrying a suitcase. The man looked down at Niamh and asked if she was alright, Mark replied, "I don't know. Please go over there and call an ambulance." As the man stepped past him, Niamh's eyes opened and she asked,

"Am I dead?"

"No, honey. You're fine. What happened?"

"I thought I saw a ghost, Mark. He looked so real."

Mark said, "Who looked so real?"

Before she could answer, the man walked back into her view, and she screamed again. The man knelt down and took one of her hands and said, "It's me, darling. I'm home." Then she fainted for the second time.

Mark looked up at the man and asked, "Who are you?"

"I'm her husband. Who are you?"

"But you're dead! You're supposed to be dead! You were killed in a fishing accident years ago. You're dead!"

The man smiled and answered, "Obviously not." Then, they both lifted Niamh off the floor and laid her on the couch. The man asked again, "Who exactly are you?"

"My name is Mark. Niamh and I are getting married."

"Married? Is that so? Niamh won't be marrying anyone as long as I'm alive; and I'm definitely alive." Mark was stunned. He didn't know what to say or what to do. He looked down at Niamh who was breathing comfortably but still unconscious. The man continued, "Look, I know it's a bit of a shock . . . "

Mark interrupted, "A bit of a shock? Ya think?? You died years ago. What happened?"

The man took a deep breath, looked down at Niamh and began explaining his history to Mark. "I grew up in the northern parts of Ireland, back when the troubles were really bad with the IRA and the British. A lot of my friends were in the militant section of the IRA and kept trying to recruit me, but I wanted no part of it. Niamh and I had just gotten married, and she was having our first child at the time. But the IRA wouldn't take no for an answer. They threatened me and they threatened to hurt or kill my wife and baby if I didn't go with them."

Then, one weekend, they had a big fight with the English when I was with the group and an English army man was killed. Everyone ran, including me, and we were all scared for our lives. Unfortunately, I was the only one there who wasn't wearing a mask. The English identified me and to make a long story short, they offered me no jail time if I would testify against my friends in the IRA. It was a no-win situation. If I didn't testify, I would've been convicted of murder, ruining Niamh's life. And if I did testify, my friends would know and would hunt me down and kill me and probably Niamh as well. The only choice I had was to turn state's evidence and accept the plea deal to enter the witness protection program."

Mark was stunned and didn't speak as he continued, "After the trial, the state made up the story about me being killed on a fishing boat. They gave me a new name and sent me to Wales to work in a factory, which is where I've been ever since. Then, last week, someone came to see me to tell that the last of the IRA bosses had died in prison from a hunger strike. There was no one left who still had a grudge against me. They told me it was my decision to keep my new identity or come back to my old home. And here I am."

Mark asked, "How much does Niamh know about this?"

"Nothing. She thought I died in a fishing accident."

"How are you going to explain it to her?"

Before he could answer that question, Niamh, who had awakened and heard the entire conversation, said, "He doesn't have to repeat it . . . I heard it all." But they did spend the next two hours going over the entire history of events. Niamh asked a thousand questions and he answered them all. Mark sat by in a stupor, never saying a word until it was clear the conversation was over. Then he asked,

"So where does all that leave things now?"

He looked in Niamh's eyes. She was looking back in his eyes as her old husband, named Gorden, answered, "It means we're still married. We're Irish and we're Catholic and in this country a man and woman stay married until one of them is officially dead. Which, clearly, I am not!"

Mark rose from the couch as the other two remained seated. He knew he couldn't stay. Gorden knew he couldn't stay. And worst of all, Niamh knew he couldn't stay. He walked out without a word, without a thought in his mind, and without a single feeling left in his battered and broken heart.

He found his car and somehow drove over to Burtonport to see his friend, Jims. Jims was the only man in Ireland he could talk to now. The only man alive who would listen to him explain things and yet, say nothing. He was the only man Mark knew who would somehow prevent him from drinking himself to death that night.

Jims took Mark to his office in the back of the pub, got them both a Guinness and let Mark start talking. Jims was a good man. He let Mark talk, and talk, and talk, until the many Guinness's and Mark's broken heart took their toll and caused sleep to finally take over. Jims laid him on the cot, covered him up, and turned off the light.

When Jims came to check on him in the morning, Mark was gone. He had risen at daybreak, got in his car, and drove up the steep cliff where he and Niamh first met. He thought, if only for a second, that it would be quite fitting to simply drive off the cliff and end it all. That one second quickly passed. Instead, he parked and stared off into the vast Atlantic, through the clouds, towards his home in North Carolina. He was wondering how he could live now, how he could exist, even how he could breathe. Niamh had been his life for so long, he didn't know any other way. He didn't want any other life. Should he go back to North Carolina?

As his mind was contemplating all these things, a raven landed on the hood of his car. As it tried to steady itself against the never-ending wind, it turned into the breeze, directly facing into the car, staring at Mark, who was staring back at it. Ravens are rather common in Europe and Ireland, so Mark wasn't all that surprised to see the bird. What did surprise him was how long the bird stared directly into his eyes, or at least it seemed as though it did. Mark wasn't entirely sure, but he thought ravens made a sound like, "Caw, caw . . ."

This one didn't. After several silent moments of staring, it hunched down and squawked loudly, "Stay" before flying off into the wind. At least, to Mark, that's what it sounded like the bird said. That settled it. He would stay. His heart might be broken, never to mend; but Ireland was his home now. He loved the people, the loved the land, the loved the culture, and unfortunately, he loved something else he could never have. But he would stay.

He drove back home and took some aspirin for his headache, then went into town for something to eat, hoping that would make him feel better. He went into the restaurant and was seated by a young lady that seemed to be miniature version of Claire. Her hair was tied tightly in a bun on top of her head. Her long dress was down to her ankles, and she was wearing no makeup at all. As he contemplated this, the real Claire came up behind him and said, "A little early for you, isn't it?"

Though he was Claire's boss, she never quite gave him the respect he thought she should. "Just bring me some pancakes and coffee, please."

"Your waitress will be right back. You can order from her." Normally, he would let this go. He knew how Claire was. But today was not a normal day.

"Claire, YOU will bring me pancakes, syrup, and coffee. Right now!" Claire was a lot of things, but she wasn't stupid. She went to the kitchen and quickly brought out his breakfast. She sat it down, then said,

"Anything else, sir?"

"No, thank you."

Then, she pulled out a chair and moved it close to him. She sat down, and said, "Okay, what's going on? And don't tell me 'Nothing!' You explain yourself right now and I'm not leaving until you do."

He took a few bites, sipped a little of his coffee, then figured she was telling the truth. She wouldn't leave. He laid his fork down, got a refill, and started. He told her everything. She listened and only asked a few questions. She might be CLAIRE#@%! But she was also Claire . . . When he finished, she got up and hugged him. He also knew that he didn't have to tell anyone else in town—Claire would take care of that.

TWELVE

UNDERSTANDABLY SO, THE NEWS OF NIAMH, Gorden, and Mark startled the town. It was the main subject of gossip and conversation for the next week. Mark tried to stay out of sight, but he still had his job to do, which wasn't easy now. When Mark told Ailen what had happened, he volunteered to help Mark do some things, but this wasn't Ailen's expertise, and his help would have made things harder for Mark. Ailen OWNED all the businesses, but Mark RAN all the businesses. Big difference!

Mark tried to stay in his office over the bar as much as he could. He knew Claire could run the restaurant efficiently, just as he knew Eileen would run the bar efficiently. The other few businesses didn't need much hands-on work either. Mark paid all the bills, ordered supplies, did the payroll, and all the other boring stuff that comes with the job . . . all the stuff Ailen didn't want to do.

After a week of trying to lay low and stay out of everyone's way, Mark was in his office working on payroll when his cell phone rang. It was Niamh. He started not to answer it, but he knew he had to.

"Hello."

"Mark, it's me. Do you hate me?"

"No! Never. You know how I feel about you. I know you didn't have any idea of what was going to happen. Did you?"

"Mark! Of course, I didn't. I was extremely more shocked that day than you were. I thought Gorden had died years ago. My heart broke back then, just as it's broken now."

Mark sat up quickly and asked, "Your heart is broken now?"

"Of course, it is. What do you think? I loved you. I still love you. How can I ever stop loving you?"

Mark didn't know what to say, except, "Really?"

"Yes, Mark! I can't turn off my feelings like a waterspout!"

"I know, but what about Gorden?"

"That's the hard part, Mark. When we were married, I loved him more than life. We had a child together and I thought our life was perfect and would last forever. Then . . . whatever happened, happened. I thought he was dead. It took me a long time to recover from that. Now he's back and I don't know how I feel. I'm glad he's alive and I'm glad my daughter will have her dad, but Mark, things are different with us." Mark didn't know what to say, so he wisely kept quiet. She continued, "It's like we hardly know each other. Even for him it's been difficult. He doesn't know if he should kiss me goodnight or shake my hand. It's very hard."

At this point, there was a two-or-three-minute silence in the conversation. Finally, Mark asked, "What are you going to do?"

He could tell Niamh was crying a little as she answered, "I don't know. According to the law and the church, we're still married. There's nothing I can do to change that. But things are different now. We both know it. Maybe time will ease things, I don't know. I don't know what to do." At this point, she started crying uncontrollably. Mark held the phone while he felt his heart melting away.

Finally, Niamh said, "I have to go." She hung up the phone while Mark kept his phone up to his ear, just in case she came back. She didn't.

* * *

Niamh and Gorden had a hard life ahead of them. All these years had created a void that was not easy to overcome. Plus, the insurance company that paid Niamh a healthy sum of money on her 'deceased' husband's life, now wanted their money back. Niamh had saved a lot of it but had also used a considerable amount of it to relocate and take care of her daughter. Gorden had nothing. He would have to find a job in the fishing industry and Niamh would also have to find something to help support them. At every turn, her life seemed to be slipping away.

Gorden was finding it just as hard to resume their lives as though nothing had happened. Neither of them could resume their feelings and their emotions from years ago. They were two people living in the same house, sharing the same life, yet miles apart from each other in every way possible. Gorden knew about Mark. He knew Niamh was in love with him, but he didn't know what to do. She was HIS wife! He started drinking each night because he didn't know what else to do. He really was a good man, caught up in a nightmare of a life, without a clue of how to continue.

Days turned into weeks, and weeks into months, as time became a torture bearer of hardship and agony for all of them. Gorden found a job on a local fishing boat making minimum wage. Niamh found employment in one of the local textile mills. She didn't call Mark again. What would she say? Every couple of weeks, Mark would see her or Gorden doing some shopping in town. If it was Gorden, he would quickly turn a corner and leave. But, if he saw Niamh . . . if he saw her, he would somehow hide behind a car, or a sign, or anything he could find, just to see her for a few precious moments.

Ailen tried to convince Mark to travel with him on some of his business trips, or back to North Carolina when they visited Gabriella's family. No, Mark didn't want any of it. He worked, he did all of his duties, he went to church every Sunday, and had a Guinness or two after work most nights. Then, he went home. He let his hair grow a bit longer and his beard became a tad more scraggly, but who cared? Only Eileen and Claire . . . and he knew how to ignore them. No, the main question he now had to answer wasn't from Eileen or Claire or Ailen, or even Jims. It was from himself.

It was only from himself. What does a man do when his heart is broken? When his dreams are shattered? When his life seems over? What does he do? What do I do?

ThIRTEEN

GORDEN AND NIAMH HAD ANYTHING BUT SMOOTH SAILING.
Neither was sure how they felt about each other. Their daughter
was the only thing keeping them from going insane. Niamh
couldn't forget or release her feelings for Mark, and Gorden
knew she couldn't. Add all this to the fact that they had no
money, were deeply in debt, and saw no light at the end of the
tunnel. Gorden's fishing job was minimum wage and Niamh's
job wasn't much better. Then, Gorden started his daily routine
of stopping off at the pub on the way home and this siphoned off
any extra money they had.

One day, Gorden's boss told him of an offer on a major fishing
boat that would nearly double his pay. However, it also meant
he would be out at sea 6-8 weeks at a time. He accepted the offer
without even discussing it with Niamh. They needed the money
and the time apart, plus, they would have to move about an hour
away, up the coast for the new job. Gorden loved this aspect of
it.

The night before the move, Gorden had once again stopped at
the pub to drown his sorrows. Their daughter was in her
bedroom packing all her things and listening to the radio. Niamh
stepped out in the yard and called Mark to tell him the news.
When Mark saw it was Niamh who was calling him, he nearly
passed out. It had been months since they'd spoken, and he knew
there was nothing that would ever change. Divorce simply

wasn't done in rural Irish life. But he had no choice. He had to answer, "Hello."

"Hello, Mark, it's Niamh."

"Niamh . . . " He didn't know what else to say.

"I know this call is very uncomfortable for you, but I wanted to tell you something."

His heart sprang up! Was she going to tell him she still loved him and was leaving her husband? That she couldn't live without him? That she was coming to see him right now? He calmed his heartbeat as much as possible and asked, "What?"

"Gorden and I are moving away. He got a new job, and we have to move up the coast about an hour away from here. We're leaving tomorrow." Mark felt as if someone had stuck a dagger through his heart. As long as she was in town, he might occasionally see her. There might be some chance of talking to her. There might be something . . . anything. But now? Nothing. So, Mark said nothing. What could he say? After several moments of silence, she asked, "Mark?"

"Yes, I'm here. I don't know what to say. Why? Where are you moving? Is this what you want, Niamh?"

"No, you know it's not what I want. We have no choice, Mark. We're broke. We have nothing, and this new job of Gorden's might actually save us."

"Do you have to go, Niamh? Can't you stay and let him go? You know how I feel. I'll never stop loving you. You know that. Isn't there any way we can work this out? Please!"

She wanted to say*, yes, I'll stay. I'll never leave you, Mark. I'll always love you*. But she knew she couldn't. Good Irish Catholic girls never divorced. It simply wasn't done. So, she answered the only way she could, "No." And she disconnected her call. Mark kept holding the phone, hoping for a miracle that would never come. Sometimes life is not fair. Gorden was not happy. Niamh was heartbroken and not happy. Mark was lost, disoriented, unredeemed, adrift, and irrevocably cast-away. Yet nothing could be done. Nothing. No matter what logic was used, it always came back to the same old thing: *the heart wants what the heart wants.*

So that night, one Irishman, who had a wife that didn't love him, got slovenly drunk. And another Irishman (by way of America) also got slovenly drunk. It didn't help either of them. One of them had his buddies drive him home. The other had Eileen drag him upstairs and lay him across the couch. Each of them would regret to see the sun rise in the morning.

* * *

Mark found the early morning especially hard. He wasn't the seasoned drinker that Gorden was. Plus, he was in Eileen's apartment, which used to be his apartment before Eileen moved in. Of course, this small fact was clouded by the remains of Sir Guinness which still altered his thinking significantly. He rose from the couch and had a tremendous urge to find the bathroom immediately, for more than one reason. This urge was so great that he forgot that this wasn't his apartment any longer, it was Eileen's. But Sir Guinness can do that at times, especially when your mind has more preeminent thoughts.

He stumbled toward the bathroom, opened the door and BAM!! . . . there was Eileen, just getting out of the shower, completely nude, reaching for a towel. She froze for half-a-second, Mark froze, well, everything except his eyes, and they both seemed unable to comprehend what had happened. Eileen was the first to act as she grabbed her towel and tried to cover up. Then Mark acted on the impulse that had taken him into the bathroom in the first place. He threw up in the sink. Eileen yelled out, "What are you doing?" But from his continuous retching, it was clearly evident what he was doing.

She raced past him with the towel covering her front. He took a one-second break in his regurgitating episode to quickly turn and glance in her direction as she passed by him. The towel didn't cover her back side. Sometimes, heaving and retching have their surprise elements. After there was nothing left to come up, he tried his best to clean the sink and the floor around him. Then he sat on the toilet and the remains of last night's calamity came out the other end. Unfortunately, Eileen's tiny bathroom didn't have a fan to whisk away the obligatory odors that come from such episodes. When he finally finished all his business, he first peeped out the door to see if Eileen was waiting for him. She was nowhere in sight, so he tiptoed out of the bathroom, slid over to the main door, and exited her apartment as quickly and quietly as he could.

Eileen was in her bedroom getting dressed when she heard the front door close. She peeped out, didn't see anyone, then went to the window to look down at the street. She saw Mark walking away in the direction of the restaurant. Then, she noticed a smell in her house . . . something had died in the walls; something old, rotten, and nasty.

Mark wanted to go home, however, that was at least another ten-minute walk, and he needed something strong and black, very quickly. He came to the restaurant and went inside to sit down at the first table he saw. Unfortunately, Claire saw him as well. She walked up to him and asked, "Do you have a reservation?" Before he could answer, she asked, "Isn't that the same shirt you had on yesterday?" Then she looked downward and said, "Is that puke on your pants?"

He meekly looked up at her and said, "Coffee, please." Instead of exploding, Claire quickly went back to the kitchen and came out with a 'to-go' mug of coffee. She placed it in front of him and said,

"Mark, I don't want to know what you did last night, but I do need you to leave the restaurant right now. You stink, you look terrible, and you're obviously still drunk."

He couldn't argue with any of that. He picked up his coffee, said, "Thank you," and started for the door. As he was just stepping outside, Claire came up behind him and asked,

"Niamh?" He only looked at her, nodded, and walked away.

As is becoming a day like this, when he took his first sip of coffee, the lid came off and it spilled down his shirt. To make matters worse, it wasn't even coffee—it was TEA! He wasn't that Irish yet, to abandon coffee for tea. He threw away the remaining contents in a trash bin and continued on his way home, but small-town Ireland came into play. He met Mrs. Mayhew on the sidewalk, and she stopped in front of him and said, "Good morning, Mark. What a beautiful . . . "But she never finished her thought, the sight of a tea-stained shirt and puke-stained pants changed her perception. She continued, "Are you alright, dear?"

"Yes, ma'am. Thank you very much. I've just had a tough morning."

"Are you sure? I could walk you home if it would help."

"No, ma'am. I'm fine. Thank you very much, though." He stepped around her and continued walking, but didn't get half a block before he met old Mr. Guarino, who stepped in front of him and said,

"Aye, I remember those days. I had a few of them meself back in me wild youth. Go on home son, have a cup of tea and you'll feel much better." He slapped Mark on the back and waved to some of his friends while pointing at Mark. Fortunately, he soon came to his apartment. All he could do was take off the soiled clothes, take a quick shower, swallow some aspirin, and fall into bed. It was going to be a long day. He laid there, unable to sleep, with his mind whirling around thoughts of Niamh. Later, as he settled a bit, he started silently singing an old Linda Ronstadt song,

Well I spent my whole lifetime
In a world where the sunshine
Finds excuses for not hangin' 'round
I squandered emotions
On the slightest of notions
And the first easy loving I found
But soon all the good times
The gay times and play times
Like colors run together and fade
Oh Lord if you hear me
Touch me and hold me
And keep me from blowing away

There's times when I trembled
When my mind remembered
The days that just crumbled away
With nothing to show
But these lines that I know
Are beginning to show in my face

Oh Lord if you're listening
I know I'm no Christian
And I ain't got much coming to me
So send down some sunshine
Throw out your lifeline
And keep me from blowing away

Oh Lord if you hear me
Touch me and hold me
And keep me from blowing away

FOURTEEN

THE WEEKS PASSED INTO MONTHS. Niamh and Gorden moved up the coast and started their new life. Mark continued to exist, though he wasn't sure how. He had an uneasy truce with Eileen after the "bathroom incident." He thought he had convinced her that he hadn't seen anything that fateful morning, that he was too sick. It wasn't easy to fool Eileen and he wasn't sure she believed his story. There were times he would look up from some work he was doing, and she would be staring directly at him, and wouldn't look away. It was very disconcerting . . . and weird.

Ailen had returned from one of his trips and he spent his free time with Mark and listened to him reminisce about the past and his struggle with the future. It was what friends did for each other. Other times, Mark would drive over to Burtonport to see Jims. Jims seldom offered any advice. He was simply a shoulder to lean on and a steady friend Mark could count on.

One evening, the town had a small celebration and Mark attended so he could think of something else besides . . . well, you know. He got his drink and found a corner to sit in by himself and enjoy people-watching, which was always good sport. Old Conner was there, drool dribbling down his chin and beard as he spoke Gaelic to anyone who would listen, while he secretly lusted over any female nearby . . . any age, any condition. Ailen and the beautiful Gabriella even made a short appearance, which nearly rendered old Conner speechless.

Mark was enjoying the evening of music and dancing until Claire made her appearance halfway through the festivities. As he suspected, she had totally abandoned her daytime, Amish costume of long dress, hair in a bun, with no makeup; and reverted to her short-dress, hair-flowing, full makeup, sexy, "look at me" manifestation of the evening. If nothing else—she WAS fun to look at, he couldn't deny that. As she walked across the floor, making sure everyone noticed her, old Conner was the first to approach her. "Cen choi en bine, maec raelict", he said to her as Claire tried to ignore him. He then grabbed her arm and repeated his Gaelic nonsense, which caused Claire to turn and stare a hole through his brain. Somehow, this action made more sense than any Gaelic words old Conner could utter. He turned and stumbled away.

Then Claire spotted Mark over in the corner, by himself. All the men in the pub, and most of the women, watched her saunter over to Mark, who knew this time would come, but he still didn't know how to handle it. When she arrived in front of him, she reached down to do something with the high-heeled shoe she was wearing, when in fact, there was nothing wrong with her shoe at all, she just wanted a reason to bend over and reveal herself, in a low-cut top, to Mark and get his interest peaked. It worked.

"Good evening, Claire. Nice to see you." She didn't answer, only smiling back in that Amish, alluring nature that was only hers to accomplish. "You're looking very nice. Is that a new dress?"

"No, Mark. I'm not going to take it off and show you the price tag—not now, anyway."

Mark should've expected this sort of response, but Claire always had a way of surprising him, and catching him off-guard. "I didn't expect you to take it off and show me the price tag, Claire. You know that."

"Oh, you want to wait to get me back to your apartment and take it off. Is that right?"

"No, Claire . . ."

"So, you want to go back to my place when I undress. Is that it?"

"Claire!"

She smiled as she answered, "So, you're saying you don't want to see me undressed. Is that correct?"

"I, umm, that's not what I said, Claire. I meant . . . umm, I meant . . . "

"Don't worry, Mark. You have no chance of seeing me undress tonight. Put your tongue back in your mouth and sip some Guinness; that's the only thing you'll be tasting tonight." Then she casually reached down and adjusted the strap on her high heel shoe, only so that Mark could get an up-close, personal view of her ample cleavage, which he did take full advantage of.

As he watched her walk away, old Conner came up to him and mumbled some sort of gibberish. Mark looked over at him, turned to walk away, and intentionally stepped on Conner's toe as he left. Only Conner saw him leave, since everyone was still watching Claire saunter through the crowd. He'd only had about half of a Guinness, so he walked back to his apartment, got in his car, and made the short drive to Burtonport. Not to visit Jims again, but to go up to the cliff and dream.

* * *

Ailen didn't get to be rich, successful, and intelligent by accident. He could sense things in business and in life, and he knew when to act. He knew Mark was sinking and he knew he had to do something to help his friend. He and Gabriella hatched a plan that would stir Mark to action. In fact, they had been planning to start a business in Winston-Salem, Gabriella's hometown, so that her family and friends would have something to operate and care for. However, instead of them going back to North Carolina, Ailen would send Mark to start up the new business. That would get his mind off Ireland and off Niamh, at least for a little while.

Ailen thought Mark might resist this attempt at manipulating his life, however, when he explained it to Mark, he jumped at the opportunity. Ailen would stay in Dungloe and manage the businesses, when in reality, Claire and Eileen would run the businesses, Ailen would simply try to stay out of the way and not make them mad. Ailen explained that it would probably take Mark about three months to open the new business in Winston-Salem, fully staff it, and make sure everything was operating smoothly.

When Mark lived in Winston-Salem, his favorite place to go was an Irish pub named Finnegan's Wake, the only Irish bar in Forsyth County. However, after Mark moved to Ireland, Finnegan's had closed due to staffing shortages during Covid and had not reopened. The beautiful Gabriella had convinced Ailen to reopen Finnegan's and now this was Mark's job: open the pub, staff it properly, and get it started on the right foot. Ailen's friend in Winston-Salem, Desmond, would handle all the necessary permits and other legal stuff that went along with this venture.

Mark left for America two days later. He stopped by the pub to give Eileen some final instructions, but she only stared at him, so he stopped. As he turned to leave, she said, "You saw me naked that day, didn't you?" It was more of a statement than a question, so he didn't answer. He walked to the door, and she said again, "Didn't you!"

This time, Mark slowly turned around, making sure there was ample distance between him and her and said, "Yes."

Instead of bar mugs flying at him and curse words being slung toward him, she slowly smiled and said, "And?"

Mark held her eyes for a moment, then smiled and nodded.

His next and last stop was at the restaurant, which he was not looking forward to. When he walked in, he didn't see Claire anywhere. He asked one of the waitresses about her and was told she was back in the kitchen. He walked back and opened the kitchen door as a waitress was coming out. Two cooks were busy frying things, and a dishwasher was loading up one of the machines. Claire saw him and yelled, "Get out." He thought she was talking to him. No, she was directing the staff to leave the kitchen so she and Mark would be alone.

"So, I hear you're leaving us."

"Only for a couple of months, I'll be back."

"I'm not too sure about that," Claire said, "you might get over there and find some floozy to hook-up with and never come back."

Mark smiled and answered, "Naw, if I was looking for a floozy, I'd stay here and hook-up with you."

At first, he didn't know if she was going to throw a frying pan at him or what. Then she smiled and said, "Sorry, you missed your one-and-only chance. You can only dream now."

He smiled back and asked, "Do you have any questions before I leave?"

"If I did, could you answer them?"

"Probably not."

They both smiled at each other and as Mark turned to leave, Claire yelled out, "Mark!" He stopped and looked back at her as she said, "Make sure you come back."

He walked toward the front door and one of the waitresses handed him a to-go cup as he left. He thanked her, then went outside, opened the top, saw it was tea, and threw it in the trash.

FIFTEEN

DESMOND PICKED UP MARK at the airport in Raleigh. He talked non-stop for the two-hour drive to Winston-Salem. Nothing much Mark could do, Desmond's wife and Ailen's wife were sisters, so he listened and dozed. Mark would be staying at Gabriella's house in the west end section of Winston-Salem, near downtown. After they unloaded the suitcases and used the bathroom, Desmond took Mark over to Trade Street where Finnegan's Wake was located. It looked exactly like Mark had remembered it: nice bar, several small tables around the main area, larger tables off to the side, and a great patio seating area outside.

All that was missing was a staff, supplies, and someone to take charge of things. Mark would start on all that in the morning. He had nearly forgotten how steamy North Carolina summers could be. Desmond had rented a car for Mark to drive, or rather a Jeep, and Mark first went to the grocery store to stock his refrigerator and house with needed items. Winston had changed a little since he lived here, but he could still find everything with no problems.

First thing in the morning, Mark called a hiring firm and told them what he was looking for. They promised to have applicants the next day. He next went to Finnegan's, turned everything on just to make sure the lights and appliances still worked, then sat at a table outside the front door to watch people pass by, as he thought of all that was in front of him. He wasn't there long when a young woman with tattoos all over both arms and legs came down the street on a motorized bicycle, stopped in front of him, and asked, "Is it open?"

Instead of answering her question, Mark asked her, "Is that a bicycle you're on?"

"Yeah, I like to get my exercise in every day."

Mark looked at the back wheel and noticed a motor. He asked her, "But isn't that a motor?"

"Yeah, so?"

"If that's a motor, how do you get any exercise?"

She looked quizzically at Mark and answered, "I still have to ride it." Mark tried to process that statement as she asked again, "Is Finnegan's open?"

"Not yet, but it will be soon."

She smiled and asked, "Are you hiring?"

"Maybe. Why do you ask?"

The girl got off her bike, stepped a little closer to Mark and answered, "I need a job. I'm an experienced waitress and bartender, and I've always loved this place. You won't find anyone better or more dedicated than me. I promise you that."

Something about the girl struck Mark. Somehow, he believed her. He stood up and said, "You're hired."

She smiled brightly and answered, "When do I start?"

"When can you start?"

"Right now!"

Mark extended his hand to shake hers and said, "Done. You're hired. By the way, are you interested in how much I can pay you?"

She looked squarely in his eyes and said, "No, I trust you. You'll be fair, won't you?"

"Yes, I will. One more thing . . . what's your name?"

"Amie. What's yours?"

"I'm Mark. Are you ready to start, Amie?"

"Yes, but I do have another question, my boyfriend is looking for another job as well. He's a bartender at one of the breweries. He moved here from Utah, met me, and loves it here. He went to college and everything. Do you think you might have something for him, too?"

"What's his name?"

"Eric. You'll love him. He's hard-working, smart, dedicated . . .
"

"Whoa, Amie. Tell him to come and see me and we'll talk. When could he start?"

"I'll call him right now. He'll be here in thirty minutes."

"Do it. Then, you and I can start working on fixing things up inside. Okay?"

Twenty minutes later, Eric arrived. After seeing Amie with all her tattoos and dyed hair (purple), Mark was shocked when Eric walked in the front door: tall, close-cropped hair, thin, with a nice smile, and very conservative looking. They certainly didn't look like a couple. Eric said, "Very nice to meet you, sir. Thank you for the opportunity and I promise, you will not be disappointed. I'll do anything you need done, work any hours or shift, never complain, or miss a day's work. I promise."

And just like that, Mark had his first two employees. The three of them started cleaning and arranging things. Mark made of list of all the food and beverages he needed to order. Eric volunteered to call all the breweries and distilleries around town, since that's what he had done at his previous job. By evening, they were all tired and extremely happy. Still, neither Amie nor Eric had asked what they were to be paid. Mark took them down the street to a local restaurant for dinner and heard more of their stories.

Amie was a Winston-Salem local and attended the N.C. School of the Arts as a dancer. She tried dancing in New York but was never comfortable in the big city and came home. However, in New York, she met Eric who was in graduate school at Fordham University. Here she was: tattooed, wild, purple hair, with not a care in world; and here's Eric: straightlaced, prim, proper, and very conservative. But they clicked. How? Unexplainable. They just did. Amie convinced him to come back to Winston and they've been together ever since.

Mark had visited New York several times and found it fascinating that Eric had gone to MBA school at Fordham University, in the heart of New York City. He asked him, "Where did you live in New York?"

Eric smiled and said, "Off Central Park East, 1320 North Columbus."

Mark said, "That's not far from Yankee Stadium. Did you go to many Yankee games when you were in New York?"

"No, I sure didn't."

Mark tried again, "How about Madison Square Garden or any Knicks games?"

Eric pursed his lips and said, "No, didn't really have time."

"I understand. How about Central Park? Isn't that a great place just to visit and walk around?"

"Mmm, don't think I've ever been there."

Mark was a little perplexed now, so he asked, "Did you visit the Statue of Liberty?"

"No."

"The Empire State Building?"

Finally, Eric perked up, "No, but I've seen it!"

"But you went to school in New York City? For two years?"

"Yep."

Mark nodded and said, "Well, let's talk about what kind of beers we want to have on tap."

* * *

The next morning, the staffing agency started sending people over to interview. Mark needed more wait staff, cooks, an accountant, kitchen staff, and general staff to make the place run properly. He wasn't comfortable with any of the dozen people he interviewed. Eric and Amie were busy getting the place ready, and they saw the applicants come and go, while listening to Mark tell them he was not having any luck. Amie said, "Would it be okay if we asked some of our friends to come by? No pressure. If you don't like them, just say so."

Mark looked over at Eric, who said, "You'll be happy. We know some great guys." The next morning, before noon, Mark had completed his hiring needs—all Amie and Eric's friends. However, he still needed to hire the most important person of all, the person who would manage the pub after Mark went back to Ireland. Mark perused several resumes, talked to some more of Amie and Eric's friends, but simply didn't feel comfortable with any of them. He needed someone with financial experience and education, like Eric; someone who had restaurant experience, like Eric; someone he could trust, like Eric.

He called Eric back to the office and said, "I want you to manage the pub fulltime. Can you do that?"

Eric stared back at Mark and replied, "You know I can, Mark. You'll never have to worry." And just like that, it was done. Instead of two or three months to get everything ready to open, Mark could see himself going back to Ireland in a couple of weeks. Desmond would be around to handle any financial issues, questions with permits, or licenses, things like that—but Mark was basically done. Ireland was calling.

Ailen had accomplished one goal: all this activity had taken Niamh off Mark's mind (during the days). However, at nights, alone in his house, things weren't quite so simple. Even though he absolutely knew he could never have Niamh, it didn't mean that he didn't want her . . . and he still wanted her. He didn't know if that would ever change. He was afraid it wouldn't.

Mark stayed for the grand opening of Finnegan's Wake, which was a great success. Eric handled things better than Mark thought he could have. The next morning, he called the airlines to find the next available flight to Ireland. He was ready for home.

SIXTEEN

MARK LANDED IN SHANNON and rented a car to make the drive home. He decided to make a side trip and visit the Cliffs of Moher, which weren't too far out of the way. If one could put up with all the tourists at the Cliffs, the scenery was spectacular. Mark parked across the street then walked over and found a secluded spot down the trail, away from the brunt of the crowds. He sat on the ground and leaned back against a rock to stare out at the vast seascape. The Cliffs ranged from 600-800' above the sea and were very popular throughout tourist season.

Mark dozed off for a bit and was awakened by the sound of someone playing bagpipes in the distance. That was enough to spur him onward toward home. As he got close, it was getting late in the day, and he wanted to stop by Burtonport and see his friend Jims before going home to Dungloe. Jims was always a great listener and Mark could tell him all about his trip to North Carolina and opening the bar in his hometown.

Usually, there might be four or five cars outside Jim's tavern, but tonight there were over a dozen cars in the lot. Must be a music night, he thought. He was right. As he entered, he saw the band near the back setting up their stage and instruments. Then he heard, "Mark! Is that you?" Jims was coming his way with a Guinness in hand and a smile on his face. Jims set the drink down and hugged Mark like the long, lost son he hadn't seen in years. Then he asked, "Where have you been, lad?"

Mark gave him the short version as they made their way over to the bar, where Mark usually sat at the end, so he could see everyone coming and going. Of course, Jims knew better than to bring up Niamh, so he kept quiet and let Mark talk about Finnegan's Wake and all he'd been doing. When he took a break, he looked toward the stage, where the band was still moving around, and asked, "Who's playing tonight? Anyone I know?"

Jims had a blank expression on his face, as if he didn't understand the question, or else, didn't want to answer it. Mark said, "Jims?"

"Mark, it's Siobhan's band, I didn't know you would be here." *Siobhan's band?* Mark thought. Seriously? A long time ago, before Mark and Niamh had found each other, Mark and Siobhan had connected in a 'friendly' sort of way, that nearly evolved into a serious relationship. It didn't evolve because Siobhan was astute enough to understand that Mark had Niamh on his mind and couldn't let her go. She wanted a relationship with Mark, they hit it off well with each other, but she knew he had other desires, and she didn't want to be the woman in the middle of whatever it was Mark had.

Mark didn't know what to say or ask Jims. He simply sat there staring at his Guinness, when suddenly he heard a voice, "Mark?" He turned to see Siobhan standing directly behind him. "I thought that was you."

"Siobhan, wow . . . it's great to see you. You look wonderful." Which was an understatement. She was probably the sexiest looking woman, with the nicest legs in the northern counties of Ireland.

"What are you doing here? Did you come to try and win me back?" She smiled provocatively as she said this.

"Umm, not really, I didn't even know you were going to be here tonight. I only came to see Jims."

"I was just kidding Mark. I heard long ago that you and Niamh finally found each other. Are you married yet?"

"No, we're not. That won't be happening." He then proceeded to tell her the short version of all his tribulations. Fortunately for her, the band needed her onstage to begin the show. As was her usual custom, she was dressed in an extremely short skirt, black stockings, and a rather tight knit shirt. Although Siobhan had a nice voice and her band played well, the biggest drawing card— by far—was the appearance of Siobhan in a short skirt. That sold more Guinness than any song they could have played.

As she started for the stage, her hand touched Mark's arm, then she dropped a business card next to his hand, and said, "Maybe I'll see you at the break." Mark and every other man in the pub watched her walk up to the stage and pick up the microphone. She knew how to walk, and she knew exactly why she was so popular.

Jims said, "Well, she sure remembers you." Mark didn't respond, so Jims added, "Do you remember her?"

Mark still didn't answer. He did rise from the barstool, took one last sip of Guinness, put the business card in his pocket, and walked out the door to his car. Instead of driving home, he drove up to the cliff where he and Niamh had first met . . . he couldn't help himself. Even though it was now dark, and he couldn't see anything, he could still remember everything. He tried to think of Siobhan and how she looked in that short skirt. He also tried to think of the past when he and Siobhan almost connected one fateful night. Then he tried to think of Eric and Amie at Finnegan's Wake and how they were doing.

He wondered how the pub and restaurant were doing and whether Claire or Eileen missed him. He thought briefly of Ailen and his wife, the beautiful Gabriella. Then he thought of Ailen's first wife, the equally as beautiful, Maired. But the problem with all these thoughts, and all these memories, and all these reminiscences was that none of them were Niamh. Then he realized that having such a good memory was both a blessing and a curse. A blessing because he remembered everything. And a curse because . . . he remembered everything.

He was so lost in thought, and so tired from the long flight over the ocean, that he soon dozed off. He didn't wake until the morning when the sun reflected off the mirror into his eyes. He stepped outside, took a few deep breaths, and relieved himself over at a nearby yew tree, before getting back in his car and driving home. He had just left the town limits of Burtonport, on the short drive over to Dungloe when he was stopped by a herd of sheep in the middle of the road. The sheep weren't moving, they were simply there, some were grazing on the sides of the road, the rest of them were just standing there. Mark honked his horn—nothing. He tried inching up close to them and honking his horn again—nothing.

Just then, a knock came on his side window. He looked over and an old man grinned at him. Mark got out of his car and man said, "Aye, I'm Roger, good morning to ye."

"Good morning, sir. Are these your sheep?"

"Aye."

Mark, trying to control his temper, said, "Could you move them out of the road? I need to get to Dungloe."

"Why?"

"Why what?"

"Why do you need to go to Dungloe?"

Mark politely said, "Because I live there, that's why."

"Oh . . . well they'll be done in a few minutes."

"Sir, I really need to get going now!"

"Aye . . . they're almost done."

Mark then asked him, "Is there another road I can take to Dungloe?"

"Are you walking or driving?" He asked.

"Driving."

The man nodded and replied, "Yes, driving will be the quickest."

Mark got back in the car, backed up a bit, then turned around to go the long way back to Dungloe. There's a difference between giving up and knowing when you've had enough.

SEVENTEEN

Mark first stopped at the pub to tell them he was back from America. There were no customers yet, only Eileen counting receipts and taking inventory, while a bartender was busy unloading the washing machine. Before Mark could sit down at the bar, Eileen had poured him a cup of coffee and was bringing it to him. She asked, "Everything good in America?"

He smiled and answered, "Everything is very good, better than I could've expected. How is everything here?"

"It's good. Didn't you think I could handle it?"

"Eileen . . . you know what I meant. I knew, and I know, that you can handle anything." She smiled but didn't respond. Then he continued, "I need someone to drive me over to the rental car place so I can turn in my car, then drive me home. Can you spare Warren for a few minutes?" Warren was the bartender unloading the dishwasher.

She nodded and called over to Warren, "Hey, how about driving Mark over to the rental car place, okay?" He smiled and started drying off his hands as Eileen looked back at Mark and said, "Try not to hit any sheep on the way over."

Mark stopped the coffee cup at his lips when he heard this. Eileen picked up a handful of paperwork and walked back to the office. He watched her walk away as Warren asked, "You ready to go now, sir?"

"Wait a minute." He walked over to the office where Eileen was now sitting and said, "Why did you say that?"

She looked up and asked, "Say what?"

"You said, 'Try not to hit any sheep . . . ' why did you say that?"

"I was just trying to tell you to be careful, Mark. Sometimes, in the mornings, sheep can be out grazing. I just wanted you to be on the lookout. That's all." Mark stood there, staring at her, saying nothing. She asked, "Are you okay?"

He didn't answer because he didn't know if he was okay or not. He thought, *how did she know about the incident with the sheep this morning?* Instead of responding, he turned and walked out, with Warren following him. He got in the car and was temporarily surprised when Warren also got in—he was still thinking about Eileen. He started the car, then looked over at Warren and asked, "Does Eileen ever surprise you with things she says? Like she knows stuff she shouldn't know?"

Warren smiled and answered, "No, sir; it never surprises me when she does that. She's an enchantress. That's what they do."

"An enchantress? What are you talking about?"

Warren turned toward Mark and replied, "An enchantress: they know things they shouldn't know. They can tell the future and explain the past. She's a good one." Mark stared at Warren but didn't respond, so Warren continued, "Don't worry about it, sir. She likes you."

"What do you mean, 'She likes me?'"

"Sir, everybody here, let me rephrase that, everybody in Dungloe knows she likes you. Are you the only one who doesn't know?"

Mark was shocked and said, "Get out!" Warren opened the car door to leave, and Mark yelled, "Not you! Just, get out! That can't be true!"

Warren closed the door and meekly said, "Oh, it's true, sir. Believe me."

They first drove to Mark's apartment to pick up his car, then went to drop off the rental car, finally, Mark drove Warren back to the pub. As Warren started to get out of the car, Mark asked, "She likes me in what sort of way?"

Warren, got out of the car, but before he closed the door, he leaned down, looked at Mark, and arched his eyebrows while pursing his lips. Then, he shut the door and walked in the pub. Mark watched him go and didn't move, or think, until a car came up behind him and honked its horn. Only then did Mark slowly pull away. He really didn't want to, but he needed to stop by the restaurant and check in with Claire.

When he walked in, he saw there were no empty tables, the place was packed. However, Claire saw him and waved him back to her office. She said something to a waitress as Mark came back to the office. When he sat down across from her, the waitress bought him a cup of tea and set it in front of him. He thanked her, for her kindness, he didn't thank her for bringing him that vile cup of liquid. Claire quickly said, "And to what do we owe this pleasure, pray tell?"

He did not want to argue . . . at all. "Is everything okay? Anything I need to know?"

"Only some bills that need to be addressed, and I had to hire a new waitress." She handed Mark a stack of paperwork and waited for him to ask her about the waitress. He didn't ask. He took the stack of bills, looked at her and said,

"Good job." He walked out, leaving his cup of tea on Claire's desk. He made it to his apartment, checked through all the mail on the floor, then went to make himself a cup of coffee as he thought about things: Eric and Amie, Finnegan's Wake, Siobhan, an enchantress, and of course, Niamh. Would he ever be able to convince his mind to change its agenda? He was pretty sure he knew the answer to that.

The next day, Mark and Ailen spent discussing all the businesses, especially Finnegan's Wake in North Carolina, while trying very hard to ignore the huge elephant in the room. It wasn't easy for Ailen. He wanted to help his friend, but he simply didn't know how. He and the beautiful Gabriella would be going back to Winston-Salem in a few weeks, and they'd check out the restaurant first-hand. All the businesses in Dungloe were doing well and Ailen was happy with that.

The following morning, Mark checked in on the restaurant, said hello to everyone, then left before Claire could catch him—it was going to be a good day. His office was in the upstairs of the pub, and he had to go there but the comment from the dishwasher, about Eileen liking him, still had him a little rattled. The more he thought about it, the less likely it seemed to be true—I mean, what does a dishwasher know?

He walked in the door and saw Eileen behind the bar. When she turned around, she had a cup of coffee and was setting in on the bar for Mark. How? Why? What . . . This time, he decided to ask her, "Eileen, did you just fix that cup of coffee for me—right now?"

"Yes. It's what you wanted, isn't it?"

"Of course, but how did you know I'd be coming in the door at this very moment?"

She smiled and said, "Because you always come in at this time, Mark. You're very predictable."

"But what if I'd stopped at the restaurant for a few minutes; or, started talking to someone outside for a while?"

96

"But you didn't, did you? You came in right now, just as you should, and I had your coffee ready, like I always do. Is there a problem with that, Mark?"

"No, thank you. I really appreciate that, Eileen." Maybe she is an enchantress. Or, maybe he's just very, very predictable. Either way, he could never figure it out. He went upstairs to his office, while thinking about her, then staring at his phone, wishing someone with red-tinged hair, a pretty smile, and the most beautiful green eyes he'd ever seen would call him again.

EIGHTEEN

NIAMH CAME HOME AGAIN TO AN EMPTY HOUSE. Her daughter was visiting a friend and her so-called husband was out somewhere in the North Sea on a fishing boat. Their life together was non-existent. He was gone 3-to-4 months at a time with his job. When he was home, they were like two strangers trying not to step on the other's toes. Neither was happy. Neither knew a solution. Neither could see a light at the end of this horrible tunnel.

It wasn't really Gorden's fault. There was simply nothing between him and Niamh now. He knew it and he didn't know how to fix it, or even if he wanted to fix it. When you know someone doesn't love you anymore, it's very hard. But when you know someone doesn't love you anymore AND they love someone else, it's almost unbearable. That's why the drinking started. It didn't help being on a boat for months at a time, with nothing to do except drink.

Niamh tried as hard as she knew how. But how do you make your heart feel something that's not there? How do you turn off feelings that ARE there? If it weren't for the job of taking care of her daughter, she'd probably have lost her mind. At least Gorden's job paid well, and they were working down the debts they owed. That was about the only good news in their lives right now.

They only had a two-bedroom apartment, so they slept in the same bed. Nothing else, sleep only; or in Gorden's case, after he returned from his nightly visit to the pub—passing out. He loved his daughter but felt like a stranger in her life as well—he just wasn't around enough to be a factor. So, he drank. Niamh and Gorden were both prisoners to this situation, prisoners with life sentences.

* * *

Mark, after a few months, began to meet Siobhan every week. He would go to where her band was playing, or they would meet for dinner and drinks somewhere—not in Dungloe. Siobhan was patient. She liked Mark but wanted to go slow to make sure that he was over whatever it was he thought about all the time. He always denied it, but she knew his mind was on Niamh . . . she knew it. Her question was this: how long would it take for him to erase these thoughts? And how long could she wait? Afterall, she wasn't getting any younger. She was still extremely attractive: long, dark hair, blue eyes, long, shapely legs, and a slim body that just wasn't the norm for women her age in Ireland. So, she was patient, for the time being.

Their dates were usually a few drinks, followed by some handholding, maybe a little kissing, and light foreplay. It stopped there. No sex. They never discussed it, but they each knew that was line they didn't want to cross yet.

Things with Eileen seemed normal, or as normal as it gets with someone who seems to know what you're thinking even before you know what you're thinking. The subject of him seeing her naked that day never came up again. But Eileen never dated anyone either. Mark never asked her about her personal life, and she never brought it up. They only had one uncomfortable moment. One day as Mark was leaving the pub for the day, Eileen said, "Tell Siobhan I said hi."

Mark immediately stopped and said, "What?"

"Tell Siobhan I said hi. That's all."

"Why do you think I'm going to see Siobhan? And how do you even know about her?"

Eileen started drying off the counter and asked, "Well, isn't that where you're going?"

He didn't want to lie to her, yet he didn't want to tell her the truth either. He didn't know what to say. He was saved when one of the bartenders called out to Eileen, "I've got an empty keg here, Eileen. Can you get another one brought out?" When she answered that question, Mark took the opportunity to hurry out the front door.

He thought, *how did she know that? How does she even know about Siobhan? How does . . .*

Claire was another story altogether. She knew there was somebody taking up Mark's time, she just didn't know who that someone was. And it was driving her crazy. So nearly every time Mark came into the restaurant, she tried to squeeze it out of him. Yesterday's conversation was typical of how she approached Mark, "What are you doing tonight?"

"Nothing."

"Well, you could do nothing here in Dungloe. Why do you always leave town to do 'nothing?'"

"I don't always leave town."

"Yes, you do! You've got a floozy somewhere, don't you?"

Mark loved having a secret that Claire didn't know, "No."

"You're lying, Mark. Who is she? Or are you paying for some female company? Is that it?"

Mark only smiled. He wouldn't let her drag him any further down this road. At this point, he would always leave, but not before giving Claire a big grin as he walked out. One night as he went to his car for the drive over to Burtonport to meet Siobhan, he noticed a car parked at the end of the street with the motor running. It was chilly that evening and the exhaust was easy to spot. Then he remembered that when he dropped by the restaurant, they told him Claire had left a little early.

Hmm . . . He pulled out slowly and watched in his rearview mirror as the other car also pulled out and followed him down the street. It didn't get close enough for him to see who was driving, but he had a good idea. Instead of turning for the road to Burtonport, he went the other way. The car continued to follow. Then he made three left turns in succession. The other car followed. Finally, he suddenly pulled off the road and quickly got out of the car and looked at the car following him.

The other car backed up, turned in a driveway and went back the opposite way. He never could see who was following him, but he knew. He knew it was Claire. From now on, he'd take extra precautions. The next day when he went into the restaurant, Claire saw him and went into the lady's restroom. He waited, and waited, and waited until she finally came out. He walked up to her and asked, "What did you do last night?"

"None your business what I do on my own time, SIR!"

"I saw you."

"So, you were peeping in my windows, were you?"

"You know what I mean, Claire."

She tilted her head upward and said, "Look, Mark, if you want to see me naked, just say so and we'll see what we can arrange."

He'd accomplished what he wanted. He turned and walked out. However, he would always check his rearview mirrors when he left town in the future.

NINETEEN

MARK HAD NOT BEEN BACK TO NORTH CAROLINA since Finnegan's Wake opened. Ailen had been there regularly and checked on things, not that he needed to. Eric and Amie were doing an excellent job running the pub. It made a nice profit each month and things seemed settled and long-term. Mark checked in with them through emails and texts, paid all the invoices, bills, and perused all the other paperwork they emailed him for final approval. He was very satisfied with the way things were going.

Then, one day, as he was sitting outside the pub enjoying a rare sunny day in Ireland, his cell phone rang. It was Eric calling from North Carolina. He was a bit startled since Eric had never called him before, only emails and texts. Mark answered, "Hello."

"Good morning, Mark. It's Eric calling from Winston-Salem. I hope you're well."

"I'm fine, Eric. What's up?" Mark was hoping there wasn't bad news accompanying this call.

"I have some great news, Mark, and I wanted to be the first to tell you. Amie has finally agreed to marry me!"

Mark always assumed it was Amie who was pushing Eric into marriage, not the other way around. Just as he assumed they were now living together. He said, "That's great news, Eric, I'm very happy for you both. Are you going to keep living in the same place with each other, or try to find something new?" Eric paused, then quickly added, "We don't live together, Mark. We have separate apartments; we want you to know that. We would never . . . well, you know . . . do that, unless we were married."

Mark quickly tried to change the subject and asked, "Great, have you thought about a date yet?"

"Oh, yes, that's why I'm calling. We want you to be here, after all, you're the reason we've become so settled and happy with our lives now. You have to be here, Mark!" That news surprised Mark, but he agreed and told Eric to simply let him know when the date was, and he would be there. Then, Eric told him, "And don't worry about the plane tickets, we've been taking donations from everyone to pay for your airfare. We have a jar at the end of the bar and people keep putting a dollar or two in each day. We have more than enough to pay for your ticket—maybe even first class!"

Mark was shocked and very happy to hear this news. Then Eric told him the final bit of information, "I also want you to be one of my groomsmen for the ceremony. Will you do it?"

A groomsman? Mark didn't know what to say. Didn't Eric have three or four friends that he could get? Anyway, he didn't want to spoil Eric's day, so he quickly said, "Yes, I'd be very happy to be one."

Then Eric added, "There'll be eight groomsmen and you'll all be wearing black tuxedos—don't worry about that either, we've saved money for the tux rentals as well. We'll get you fitted when you get here." Mark thought, *eight groomsmen?* Then Eric added, "And, of course, Amie will have her eight bridesmaids as well. It's going to be a great day, Mark!"

Then Erik continued to tell Mark all the details, entirely more details than Mark really wanted to hear, but he was happy to listen to the joy and happiness in Eric's voice. He finally told him the dates for the wedding and for the pre-wedding parties and everything else. When Mark ended the phone call, he was exhausted just listening to everything, and his coffee was cold— a small price to pay for all the joy in the lives of Eric and Amie.

Ailen paid for Mark's airfare and told Eric to keep the money they'd been saving as a wedding present. Dang, Ailen is a nice guy—not First Class nice, but nice. Mark arrived in Winston-Salem and settled in at the beautiful Gabriella's house in the west end. He went to all the pre-wedding events and met all the other people in the wedding. He was not surprised at all at what he'd seen.

The other seven groomsmen could have been clones of Eric. All were about the same size, all had very conservative haircuts, all looked like you'd expect your banker to look. Amie's friends were a bit different. Each of the eight Maids of Honor had a different color hair and hairstyle, ranging in length from below waist level, to bald on the sides with a blue mohawk. But they were all nice and extremely happy for Eric and Amie.

The ceremony was performed by a preacher dressed in a t-shirt, flip-flops, and cutoff blue jeans, named Randy. No last name, just Randy. Incredibly, he was Eric's childhood friend, and had become ordained just so he could marry them. The ceremony was a tale-of-two-cities. All the groomsmen were very boring in their black tuxedos, whereas the bridesmaids all had on different colored gowns that matched their hair. The same could be said of the congregation: the right side was very conservative: suits and ties, and pale looking dresses. While the left side was dressed in every color in the rainbow, ranging from long-flowing pink dresses to micro-mini skirts that left little to the imagination.

However, Randy did a wonderful job with the nuptials, Eric and Amie said their "I do's," and the happy couple invited everyone back to Finnegan's Wake for the afterparty. Mark made an appearance and spoke with everyone, then eased out the back door and walked down the street. Happy for his friends, but a sense of melancholy overwhelming him as he thought that his chances of a day like this were as foggy as an early Irish morning.

He started down Trade Street and turned right on Fourth Street as he walked aimlessly through Winston-Salem, trying not to start crying, or even worse—start drinking. To take his mind off these thoughts, he took out his cell phone and called Dungloe to check on things. He called Claire first and she answered, "Aren't you still in America?"

"Yes, I was just calling to check in."

"You don't think I'm smart enough to run things for a few days while you're gone?" Before he could respond, she continued, "Or, you wanted to see if I was just coming out of the shower? Which is it, Mark?"

"Claire, I . . . "

She interrupted and said, "Well, you're right, I did just get out of the shower. I just now dried off but haven't had the chance to start dressing yet. Do you want to do a video call?"

Mark's mind started spinning. *Was she telling the truth? How could he believe her? Finally, how do I make a video call?* Then, she said, "Goodbye, Mark. Sweet dreams." And she disconnected the call.

He found a bench to sit on outside a coffee shop while he wondered if he should call Eileen or not. After the call with Claire, he wasn't sure. While he was thinking, an older woman walked up to him and asked, "Can I get you anything, sir?" At first, he didn't know what she was referring to, then he realized that she was a waitress for the coffee shop.

He answered, "Oh, yes, a cup of coffee, please."

"Regular, decaf, espresso, café latte, mocha, or iced coffee?"

He couldn't think . . . what kind of place was this? He changed his mind and answered, "Just bring me a Coke."

"Regular Coke, Diet Coke, Coke Zero, Vanilla Coke, or Cherry Coke?"

His mind was so confused, he just got up and walked away. He thought he heard the waitress say something inappropriate, but he wasn't sure. He started walking and his mind kept repeating, *Niamh, Niamh, Niamh, Niamh, Niamh.* He couldn't stop his mind from saying her name. He couldn't stop thinking about what could have been. He couldn't stop . . . he just couldn't stop. Before he realized where he was, he'd arrived at Hanes Park, away from downtown and miles from where his car was parked.

He found a secluded bench in the park to sit on and started singing an old Doobie Brothers' song to himself, as he thought of Niamh,

I'm sittin' in my room, I'm starin' out my window
And I wonder where you've gone
Thinking back on the happy hours just before the dawn
Outside the wind is blowin'
It seems to call your name again
Where have you gone

City streets and lonely highways
I travel down
My car is empty and the radio just seems to bring me down
I'm just tryin' to find me
A pretty smile that I can get into
It's true, I'm lost without you

He cried a little, then he dreamed. After an unknown period of time, a little blue bird landed on the bench next to him, breaking his thoughts. As the bird flew away, Mark decided to call Eileen and check with her. She answered his call, "Hello, Mark, calling to check in and see how things are?"

"Umm, well . . . "

"Well, everything is fine. I'm pretty busy here, so I'll let you continue your bird watching." And she hung up.

Mark stared at his phone. He wanted to call her back and ask . . . then he thought, *nope.*

TWENTY

THE DAY AFTER THEIR WEDDING, Eric and Amie were back at work. Mark tried to convince them to take a few days off, at the least, but they wouldn't hear of it. Amie said, "Mark, you trusted us to run the business and we're not going to let you down." Eric nodded in agreement. Mark learned early on that Eric always agreed with everything Amie said . . . always! So, he booked his flight back to Ireland and went home to pack. He couldn't find a flight until the following night, so he decided to go downtown to a bar where no one knew him, and he could brood in private.

He found an interesting place near the Innovation Quarter. It was a brewery that was connected to an Italian pizza place—good combination. He sat inside at the far end of the bar, by himself. As he started on his second local brew, people were coming in and the place started to fill up. Some people were looking for the newest brew-of-the-month, others looking for a mouth-watering pizza. Most wanted both.

As Mark finished his second beer and wondered if he should go home or try one more, someone spoke to him, saying, "Did you like the Ardmore Amber?" Which was the name of the local brew he had just finished. At first, he didn't understand the question, then looked at his empty glass, which had Ardmore Amber printed on it.

He looked over and saw a young lady, at least a few years younger than him, sitting on the stool next to him. She asked again, "Did you like it?"

"Yes, it was good."

She smiled and turned on the stool to face Mark, adding, "I've never tried it but have always wanted to." As she said this, Mark couldn't help but notice that she was wearing an exceptionally short skirt that was proving to be very inadequate in the job of covering the young lady's lovely legs. She continued, "Would you recommend it?"

"Well, I enjoyed it."

She smiled again and said, "That's good enough for me. Looks like it's a 6.5%, that's pretty strong, hope I'll be able to drive myself home afterward." Mark nodded, not totally understanding what she meant by that statement. Then she smiled widely at Mark and added, "If I have two of them, I know I won't be able to drive home."

Again, Mark nodded and was thinking, *I wonder what the alcohol percentage of Guinness is?* The bartender came by, and the young lady said, "I'll have what he's having." When the bartender left, she reached over and said, "My name's Anne." Mark shook her hand and thought, *I wonder if that's with an E on the end, or not?* Then, she asked, "What's your name?"

"Oh, it's Mark."

She leaned closer to him and said, "Come to think of it, Mark, I think I have a few of these Ardmore Ambers in my fridge at home. Would you like to come with me, and see?"

"No, I probably shouldn't have another one, I have an early flight tomorrow. Thanks anyway, Anne."

Anne's smile disappeared instantly. She got off the stool and walked toward the restroom area. The bartender walked up with the beer she'd ordered, and Mark said, "I think she went to the bathroom."

The bartender asked, "You think she went to the bathroom? Really?"

"Yeah, she should be right back." The bartender nodded at Mark but didn't respond. Several minutes later, Mark saw Anne walking out of the bar with a well-dressed man, who Mark thought was probably her brother, or a close friend. He decided not to have another Amber and closed out his bill. Time to go home and pack. And think.

* * *

The flight back to Ireland was long and uneventful. However, the weather in Ireland was quite different than in North Carolina. Cool, misting rain, with a low cloud cover; as opposed to hot, humid, and sunny in Winston-Salem. Mark loved them both. He made it back to Dungloe with no problems and finished unpacking all his things when his phone rang. The phone in his apartment, not his cell phone. He answered, "Hello."

"Mark, are you coming in today?" It was Eileen.

"Yeah, I'm already here, got back this morning."

"I know you're back, Mark. I was asking if you're coming into the pub today."

Then he realized that she had called him on his apartment phone, not his cell phone. How did she know he was back? So, he asked her, "How did you know I was in my apartment?"

"Mark, what difference does that make? I just need to know if you're coming into the pub or not. I have something you need to look at. Are you coming or not?"

But he wanted to know HOW she knew he was in his apartment. He hadn't told anyone of his plans. No one had seen him arrive.

How did she know? So, he started to ask again, "But, how did you . . . " The line went dead. Eileen hung up. He stood there looking at the receiver in his hand, thinking, *how does she know this stuff?* He finished up everything and brushed his teeth before changing into a fresh shirt. Just then, his cell phone rang. It was Claire. He answered and she said, "When are you coming back? Ailen's not here and you're not here and we need to have some stuff done, Mark."

"I'm back now. I'll be over in a few minutes." There was a moment of silence before Claire spoke again,

"Well why didn't you tell me you were back so I could get ready? Seriously, Mark, sometimes I don't think you ever use your brain at all."

He replied, "Well, Eileen knew I was back."

Another moment of silence, then Claire asked, "Are you shagging her?"

"No, I'm not shagging her. Are you crazy?"

"Well how did she know you were back? There's something going on, isn't there? Don't deny it, Mark!"

He started to respond to her accusations, but instead, he decided to let her wonder. Then added, "I'll see you in a few minutes." He disconnected the call and turned his phone off before she could call back. It felt good.

He stopped by the restaurant first and gave the okay for some invoices and made a couple of phone calls to suppliers and everything was back on schedule. Claire ignored him. He had one of the servers bring him a cup of coffee in a to-go cup as he left for the bar and Eileen. Before he actually reached the pub, he stopped and thought to himself, *Every time I come into the pub, she has coffee waiting for me. Now, since I have this coffee with me, will she still have coffee waiting for me?"* Ha! He had her beat, now.

He walked in the door and looked on the bar—nothing. He looked behind the counter—nothing. He spotted the coffee pot turned off and unplugged. Just then, the bartender asked, "Anything you need sir?"

He reasoned that Eileen didn't really know WHEN he was coming, so that's why there was no coffee made for him. He felt good about that. So, he answered the bartender's question, "No, I'm good, just thought I'd pop in and surprise Eileen."

He looked at Mark and said, "Oh, it's no surprise, she told us you'd be here any minute."

Mark asked, "She told you I'd be here any minute?"

"Yes, sir."

Mark asked, "If she knew I was coming, why isn't the coffee maker turned on?"

At that moment, Eileen had walked up behind Mark and answered, "Because you already have a coffee, Mark. How many do you need?"

"But you didn't know I already had a coffee with me. You didn't know that, Eileen!" The bartender was now intrigued by this conversation and was anticipating the answer as much as Mark was.

Eileen, looked first at Mark, then at the bartender, and replied, "Mark, there are always flowers for those who want to see them." Then, she turned to walk back to the office as she waved for Mark to follow her. He turned to look at the bartender who started nodding, and said,

"Yep, she's right, sir."

TWENTY-ONE

LIFE ROLLED ON. Music played in the pub each night. Claire showed her temper. Eileen always knew what Mark was thinking or doing. Ailen popped in and out as he and the beautiful Gabriella saw fit. Siobhan and Mark had a few dinners-- nothing serious. She still knew Mark's mind was elsewhere. Jims was always available when Mark needed to brood or reminisce. And it rained. The grass became greener, with more subtle shades of green than anywhere else on earth.

Amie and Eric had altered the menu at Finnegan's Wake to make it seem even more Irish and were trying to convince Mark to buy the vacant store beside Finnegan's and expand the restaurant. Business was great! Everyone was living. Everyone was content. Everyone was comfortable . . . except Niamh.

Her life was not happy, not blissful, not loving, and not much of anything but miserable. How could it not be? She was married to a man she didn't love, a man who was ever-increasingly married to the bottle rather than to her. She was lonely, depressed, and very unhappy. The only thing that kept her from drowning was the life of her daughter. She was vicariously living her own life through her daughter now: school activities, church activities, her friends, her interests—everything! Niamh, personally, had nothing. She dreamed. She tried not to, but she couldn't help it. Life can be cruel at times.

It was not much better for her husband, Gorden. His work would keep him at sea for a month or two, which he was grateful for. It wasn't any fun for him to be at home with a wife who didn't love him. He tried. They tried. But you can't invent love. You can't make it happen. So, he drank on the boat at sea and in the pubs when he was home. Each night, he consumed every form of alcohol available. He didn't care. He was as miserable as Niamh was. Neither of them could see a way out. Both were stuck in a life that seemed like a prison. Yes, life can be very cruel at times.

One evening, when Gorden was not at sea, he went into his favorite pub and ordered an Irish whiskey. The owner of the small pub brought it to him and said, "You know you're killing yourself, right?"

Gorden downed the shot and held up the glass for another one and answered, "So?"

"You want to die? Is that right?" Gorden downed his second shot and didn't answer. The bartender filled his glass for the third time as Gorden stared at his reflection in the mirror behind the bar. He thought to himself, *Do I? Do I want to die?* Then he started thinking, or at least the whiskey started thinking for him. He thought of his days in Wales when he was in the witness protection program. He enjoyed that anonymous life. He had friends, he worked in a job he enjoyed. And, most importantly, his existence didn't make his wife and daughter miserable, like it does now. He started comparing his two lives: during the witness protection and after he came back. During the witness protection period, he was happy, he had a lot of friends, and a job he enjoyed. Plus, Niamh was happy and in love—not with him, but she was happy and in love.

Now, after he's come back, he's very unhappy, working at a job he doesn't like, and Niamh is miserable, with neither of them even remotely tasting love. He downed another shot of whiskey and thought, *Why did I come back? What have I done?* Then, another shot of whiskey, and another, then darkness. Thank goodness for the darkness. How else could he bear the light?

Somehow, Gorden woke up on the couch in his home. He didn't remember going home, as he didn't most nights. He was alone. His daughter was at school and Niamh was out somewhere . . . anywhere. He first went to bathroom to throw up and take a shower, then he stared at himself in the mirror, and said out loud, "What are you doing? Why are you here?"

He made himself a cup of tea and tried to remember where he'd hidden the contact number for the British official in the witness protection program. It took him several minutes, but he found the number. The man had told him to call if he ever needed help with anything. Gorden needed help.

When he called the number, there was no answer, so Gorden left a message asking him to call him back. Then he sat on the couch thinking *Why would he ever call me back? They don't need me anymore.* And his phone rang. It was him. Gorden immediately started lying to the official, telling him that remnants of the IRA had heard about his release and were making inquiries about his life and, more importantly, his family's lives. He made it sound very dramatic and threatening.

The official asked Gorden what he wanted him to do. He answered, "Put me back in the program. Take me back to Wales, my old life there. I never want to come back here and put my wife and child in danger. Take me back, now!" The official told Gorden he'd have to check with his superiors and see if it was possible, but he'd get back with him soon.

That afternoon, a different official called him back and asked only one question, "This would be permanent. Are you sure you want to do it?"

"Yes, I am very sure. When can you arrange it?"

Gorden was surprised to learn that someone would pick him up at the edge of town that evening. He was to bring nothing with him and tell no one what was happening. He'd just be gone. Disappeared. And the local police department would do a preliminary investigation but would not alter things. The official reason for his disappearance would be that he was drinking, walked out on the pier, and fell in the ocean. The tide would have swept him out to sea.

That night, after Niamh and his daughter were in bed, he silently went back into his house and looked at them asleep in their rooms. He wept. Then, he turned and left to meet the official on the outskirts of town. He would never be back.

Niamh woke the next morning and checked on her daughter, who was still asleep, then she looked on the couch, expecting to see her husband, sleeping off another drunken night. She still wasn't too concerned. He was probably at the bar in the back room, too drunk to come home.

When he still hadn't arrived by noon, she called his favorite pub, then another pub, then another. Nothing. No one had seen him or had any idea where he would be. She checked his closet, and all his clothes and possessions were just as he had left them. Maybe he was locked up. That had to be where he was, too drunk to even walk home and the police locked him up. She called the local Garda office and was told they did not have her husband and hadn't seen him at all.

She still wasn't overly concerned. He was somewhere sleeping it off, she was sure of it. However, when he still hadn't appeared by that evening, she then became worried. She called the Garda and reported him missing. Since it had been over twenty-four hours since he'd been seen, they told her they would check into it. When learning that his staff was scouring the neighborhood for a missing man, the chief suggested they check the local piers.

At the second pier they investigated, they found a small sailboat missing. They took the policeboat and began scanning the coast. Finally, someone spotted a stranded sailboat out in the ocean, drifting aimlessly, unoccupied. They towed it in, and after checking all other options, they fingerprinted portions of the boat. There, they found Gorden's prints—just as he had left them, per instructions from his contacts.

The police and local shipyards did a search of the coasts and areas near the shore. Nothing. They learned that the tide had been going out to sea all night. Anything, like a body, that had fallen into the water would be miles and miles out in the ocean by now. The Garda assured Niamh they would continue to search, but all indications were that her husband was probably drunk, got in the small boat, and had fallen overboard, then was swept out to sea by the current.

They did a limited search for a couple of days, but everyone knew he was gone. Everyone knew Gorden was never coming back. His daughter cried. Niamh cried a little, as well. As much as their troubles were, she certainly didn't want him to die. So, after a couple of days, she started arranging the second funeral for her husband, Gorden. Hoping that somehow his body would wash ashore or be spotted by a fishing boat someday soon. She did not want to relive her previous experience a second time.

TWENTY-TWO

AFTER THE FUNERAL, Niamh decided to move back to Dungloe . . . not because it's where Mark lived, but because it's where her parents lived, and they could help with her daughter. In fact, she hesitated in making the decision to move back because of Mark. She didn't want to put any pressure on him to resume their relationship; after all, it had been over a year, and he'd probably forgotten about her. People have crazy thoughts in times of despair. She was certain he'd be involved with some other woman, and she didn't think she could stand the thought of living with that. However, anything that concerned grandchildren, Niamh knew that grandparents ruled. They would move back.

The same house she'd moved out of was still vacant. The economy was not booming in the northern sections of the Republic of Ireland. Her parents helped her with the down payment and paid for all the moving expenses as well. They'd have done anything to have their granddaughter back where she belonged. Niamh's mother was also a very astute woman. She knew how to arrange things and get the ball rolling, without anyone knowing she was the force behind the ball rolling.

When it was decided that Niamh was moving back to Dungloe, her mother made her weekly shopping trip into town a couple of days early. Normally, she would visit the same few shops each week and go back home. She never, NEVER, went into the restaurant where Claire worked, but she knew of Claire. Everyone in Dungloe knew of Claire!

She walked into the restaurant and was seated at a table where she ordered a scone and a cup of tea, while she surveyed the scene. It wasn't hard for her to pinpoint Claire. She was the one giving all the orders. She knew of Claire's reputation and was planning on working it to her advantage. When she finished her scone and tea, the server brought her the bill. She fumbled in her purse and then exclaimed, "Jesus, Mary, and Joseph! I've forgotten my wallet."

The young server looked at her but didn't know what to say, so she said, "Hold on a minute, let me get the manager." So far, so good.

Claire came to the table and asked what the problem was, "I seem to have forgotten my purse and I don't have any money with me. If you don't mind, I'll just run home and be back in about twenty minutes."

Claire didn't recognize her, so she asked, "Do you live here in Dungloe?"

"Oh, yes, maybe you know my daughter, Niamh."

Of course, Claire knew Niamh, so she responded, "Certainly ma'am. I hope Niamh and her husband are doing well. Look, don't worry about the bill. Niamh was a friend of mine. It's the least I can do."

Claire opened the door just as expected, "Oh, I'm afraid things aren't well at all. Niamh's husband died in a fishing accident, and she has moved back here to Dungloe. I'll be sure to tell her how kind you have been about the bill. Who can I tell her has been so kind to me?" Claire was momentarily stunned, and it's not easy to stun Claire. When Claire didn't answer right away, she asked again, "And what is your name?"

"Claire. My name is Claire. You say Niamh's husband has died?"

"Yes, ma'am. Unfortunately, so."

"And Niamh has moved back here, to Dungloe?"

"Yes, she has. In fact, she's moved back into the same house she had before." At this statement, Claire walked away from the table and went into the back room. Niamh's mother knew she had accomplished her goals. She also got up and left the restaurant. She wanted to be home when things started happening.

Claire grabbed her coat and ran out the front door, nearly knocking over an elderly gentleman who was trying to come in the door. She ran down the street to the pub, where she knew Mark was located. When she came in, she saw Eileen and the bartender casually cleaning the bar area. She walked up and demanded, "Where is Mark?"

Eileen also knew how to push people's buttons, especially Claire's, so she answered, "Mark who? I'm not familiar with that name."

"Don't mess with me, girl. You'll regret it to your dying day."

Eileen smiled and asked the bartender, "Do you know anyone named Mark?" The bartender knew where his bread was buttered, so he answered,

"No ma'am. I don't know anyone named Mark."

Claire was fuming and yelled out, "Eileen! It's important! Where is he?"

Mark heard all the fuss and loud voices, of which he recognized Claire's above the others, and he came out of his office and said, "What's going on here? What's wrong, Claire?"

Claire collected herself, then calmly said, "Niamh's back in town."

"So? Why should I care if she's back here visiting her mother?"

Claire took a moment to let the suspense build, before continuing, "She's not visiting her mother. She's moved back here to the same place she had before."

Mark thought that was a bit odd. He knew her husband didn't like it here. But he could tell Claire had more to say. He asked, "So?" Claire looked down at her fingernails, and asked the bartender for a cup of tea before Mark demanded, "Claire! What?"

"Her husband is dead. He died in a fishing accident and that's why Niamh moved back." Mark stared at her for several seconds to make sure she was telling the truth. Claire expected to be grilled repeatedly about all she knew—she was looking forward to it. Instead, Mark ran out the front door without saying a word.

Eileen looked at Claire and asked, "For real?"

"As I stand here before you." When she said that, Mark burst back in the door, ran upstairs to his office, and five seconds later, ran back down the stairs, and out the door again. Claire looked at Eileen, who said,

"He forgot his keys."

Mark was so flustered, he mistakenly started on the road over to Jim's pub in the next town. When he realized what he was doing, he tried to make a U-turn on the small, Irish road—never a good idea. When he pulled off the road, into what he thought was some high grass, his car jolted to a stop and turned off. He tried the switch repeatedly, but nothing worked. It wouldn't start. He got out and looked at the front of the car to see that he had hit an old anchor, from a boat, that someone had left lying on the side of the road. The tip of the anchor had pierced the front of Mark's motor, causing serious damage.

He again tried to start it, but this time nothing happened at all, not even a sound. He reached in his pocket to call Eileen to come and pick him up before realizing he'd left his phone in the office. No car, no phone . . . he almost panicked. Then, he started running back to town. He hadn't driven that far. It shouldn't take long. Wrong. When you haven't run in a long while, and you're in your street shoes, and you're panicking-- running is hard. Very hard. He lost his breath quickly, so he tried to walk as fast as he could.

When he made it back to town, Eileen was standing in front of the pub. When he got close to her, she said, "Let's go." This was one time he didn't care how she knew. He didn't want to know how she knew. He was just glad that she did know. He was silent as Eileen drove him out to Niamh's house on Sky Road. His mind was buzzing. He couldn't think. He couldn't speak. He couldn't do anything. When she pulled in the driveway, he looked over at her but couldn't say anything. She looked at him and said, "Go. Get in there."

Mark ran up to the door and knocked three times, his lucky number. No answer, Eileen was waiting in the car just to make sure things were okay. Mark knocked four times. No answer. Eileen honked her horn and waved for Mark to come back to the car. She said, "I thought I saw some movement in the back yard. Go around back."

Mark started for the back yard, just as Niamh, who heard a car horn, was walking to the front yard. As the each turned the corner of the house, they nearly ran into each other. When Niamh realized who it was, she fainted. Mark caught her before she fell to the ground and carried her inside through the back door. He laid her on the couch and went into the kitchen to get a wet towel, but it was unnecessary. She was sitting up as he came back. She tried to stand but was unable to. Mark sat down beside her, and they held hands. Mark finally asked, "Is it true?"

She nodded and started crying, then put her arms around Mark's neck. Ten seconds, ten minutes, ten hours, later—Mark didn't know, he pulled back and asked, "Do you love me?"

She still couldn't speak, but she nodded, and kissed him passionately before she started crying again. When she stopped, Mark pulled back and said, "We're going to get married." Niamh nodded quickly and hugged him again. Mark pulled back once more and said, "Now. Tomorrow. We're getting married tomorrow." He expected some negotiation from her, but instead, she finally spoke and said,

"Yes."

TWENTY-TbREE

THAT NIGHT, AFTER NIAMH WAS FEELING BETTER, they called the local preacher, GC, who was also Mark's close friend. Excitedly, they told him they wanted to get married the next day and asked if he could perform the ceremony. GC took a deep breath and gave them the bad news. In Ireland, if you want to get married, you must give three-month's notice in person, at a civil registration office. There was silence on both ends of the call. Finally, GC asked, "Mark, did you hear me?" Still no answer, "Mark?"

"Yes, I'm here. Three-month's notice?"

"Yes."

"Why?

"That's the law, Mark. I'm sorry."

"I'll call you back." Mark hung up the phone and explained everything to Niamh, who seemed like she might start crying again. She said,

"Mark, I can't wait three months. Something will happen—I know it will. We've got to find another way. How about getting married in France, or Germany, or Italy? Could we do that?"

Mark had no idea what the marriage laws were in France, or any other country in the world, but he did know what the laws were in North Carolina. He looked in Niamh's eyes and said, "We're going to North Carolina."

Niamh held her breath as she asked, "Why?"

"Because we can get married in North Carolina as soon as we get off the plane."

Niamh screamed, "Are you sure, Mark? Don't joke with me about this."

"I'm not joking. We can do it. Will you go?"

"Of course, I'll go. When?"

They both stared at each other, then started discussing details. Who will keep Niamh's daughter? Will it be okay with Ailen? Will the restaurant and pub and other businesses be okay? What will Niamh's parents say? However, the bottom line was, regardless of the other questions, they were going to North Carolina to get married. They began calling everyone. Niamh's parents first, who were overjoyed at the news. Ailen second, who was overjoyed at the news, JIms third, who was overjoyed at the news, Eileen next, who tried to act overjoyed, and did a good job with her act. Then, there was Claire.

Mark was not looking forward to this phone call, so Niamh volunteered. When Claire answered and Niamh explained that they were going to get married immediately, Claire said, "You can't. There's a three-month waiting period." Niamh explained that in North Carolina there was no waiting period. Claire asked, "Is that legal? Will the marriage be honored here in Ireland?" Niamh froze.

She looked at Mark and asked him that question. Mark had no idea, but he said, "Yes! Completely legal." Niamh and Claire both screamed in the phone, and Niamh started crying again. As soon as the call ended, Mark called GC and asked him that question. GC assured him that any marriage performed in the

United States would be legal and completely honored in Ireland. They were going to North Carolina.

After lots of crying and kissing and hugging and explaining things to Niamh's daughter, who loved Mark, he next called Eric and Amie in Winston-Salem. He needed their help. Amie answered the phone and Mark told her that he was coming to North Carolina to get married. She said, "Getting married to who? I thought you said you weren't seeing anyone."

"To Niamh. The love of my life."

Amie said, "Are you sure, Mark? This is awfully sudden. Maybe you should take a little while and think about it. I mean . . . "

Before she could finish, Mark explained, "Amie, I've loved Niamh for over three-hundred years. We know each other better than any two people have ever known each other. This will be the most perfect marriage in the history of marriages."

A few seconds of silence passed before she said, "Let me go find Eric so you can tell him the news." When Eric got on the line and finished his congratulations, Mark explained what he needed them to do.

"I know you and Amie go to church there in Winston-Salem. Can you see if your preacher will perform the ceremony for us? Nothing fancy, just quick and legal. You can be my best man and Amie can be Niamh's, whatever you call it. Okay?"

"Yeah, no problem, I'm sure he'll do it. Now, we're Moravians. Is that okay with you?"

Mark thought, *Moravians? What's that?* So, he asked Eric what Moravians were.

Eric started to give Mark the entire history of the Moravian church and what their beliefs and thoughts were, but he correctly concluded that Mark did not want to hear all that, and quickly explained, "We're sort of like Quakers, just not as weird."

That was good enough for Mark. Eric would arrange things with the preacher, Amie would handle the wedding affairs, and Ailen had already told them that he would arrange the airplane tickets. Mark and Niamh were going to America to get married!

* * *

Ailen couldn't find first-class tickets available the next day, but he did get them the following day. Mark had never flown first-class before and Niamh had never flown anywhere before. It would be quite an adventure. Ailen drove them to Shannon to catch the flight. He expected Niamh to be a nervous wreck: getting married, first-time leaving Ireland, going to America, her first time in an airplane. He was wrong. Niamh was as calm and steady as a rock. Mark was the one who was not able to sit still on the ride to the airport or stop talking.

On the 2 ½ hour drive to Shannon, Mark told stories from his youth, then stories of college, and stories of travelling in the western United States, and details of his first arrival in Ireland. Ailen was driving and pretended to listen intently, while Niamh's mind was a thousand miles away, but it seemed to Mark like she was loving his tales.

On arrival, Niamh hugged Ailen, then Mark hugged him and thanked him for everything he'd done. They made it through customs and check-in and had about two hours before the flight left. Only then did Niamh show signs of nervousness. She asked, "It is safe, isn't it Mark?"

"Very safe. Safer than driving your car on the freeway."

She nodded, before asking, "What if something happens? Are there parachutes for everyone?"

"Nothing is going to happen. We'll be fine."

She nodded again and asked, "But what if terrorists are on the flight and they try to blow up the plane?"

"All passengers are checked. Remember when we went through security. No one can bring anything on the airplane."

"But what if the pilot has a heart attack or something?"

"There's always a copilot on board who can take over, and the navigator, engineer, and chief attendant are all qualified to fly the plane. We'll be fine." He made up this last part just to make her feel better.

She nodded again and asked, "But what if we run into a storm and get lost or get hit by lightning?"

"I checked the weather, everything is clear all the way to America." He hadn't checked the weather either.

She started again, "But,"

"How about a drink? Can I bring you back a Coke or something?"

Niamh looked back at him and said, "Yes, a Coke, with whiskey . . . lots of whiskey!"

Once they were airborne, Niamh settled down. Or maybe it was the whiskey that settled her, but either way, she was fine. First class was different. The passengers were continually offered food, drinks, and amenities that regular coach passengers weren't privy to. Plus, the seats in first class leaned back to simulate a small couch or lazy boy recliner. Whatever Ailen had paid for these tickets was more than worth it to Mark. He loved it. The only thing he loved more was having Niamh next to him, holding his hand, rubbing his arm, her foot touching his foot. All this was much, much better than any of the luxuries in first class.

They each took a short nap and were a bit surprised when the plane landed in Raleigh. They were a little disappointed they hadn't been able to sample the other luxuries of the first-class cabin. They gathered their bags and waited for the crew to start the deboarding process. Niamh was extremely excited, until the door opened, and she started walking down the gangway into the terminal. It felt as though she had entered the gates of Hades! The heat almost made her faint. Ireland never has this type of weather. Ireland never has this humidity. She looked back at Mark and said, "What is this?"

Mark smiled and replied, "Welcome to North Carolina, honey."

TWENTY-FOUR

ERIC HAD ARRANGED FOR HIS CLOSE FRIEND, and cook at Finnegan's, to pick up Mark and Niamh in Raleigh and drive them to Winston-Salem. He was a young guy named Sam who barely looked old enough to drive. He grabbed their luggage for them and led them through the terminal to his car, parked nearby in a parking deck. Much to their surprise, Sam was driving a new BMW. He loaded their bags in the trunk, and Mark and Niamh both got in the back seat, which Sam thought was a little odd, but he knew Mark was the boss, so he didn't say anything.

As they drove on the Interstate towards Winston-Salem, Mark thanked Sam for coming to pick them up, and asked him if the car was his.

"Yes, sir. I bought it earlier this year. I've always wanted a Beemer." Niamh had no idea was a *Beemer* was, but she did wonder how such a young guy could afford to buy such an expensive car. Mark wondered that as well, but didn't want to get too personal with the young man, so he asked,

"I understand you're a cook at Finnegan's Wake, is that right?"

"Yes, sir. I started a little while back, just part-time, as I'm available. I love it. We're all so happy that you reopened the place."

Mark's curiosity was peaked now . . . he'd only been working a short time and parttime, yet could buy a BMW? So, he asked, "Is this your parent's car?"

"Oh, no. It's mine, bought and paid for. It's used, though, not brand new." To Mark and Niamh, it looked right off the showroom floor. Sam could tell they were perplexed at how such a young man could afford such an expensive car, so he explained to them, "I won the money in a golf tournament and used that to buy the car."

Mark was relieved, "A golf tournament? Wow, I don't understand. I thought you were a cook at the restaurant."

"Oh, I am, sir. Eric lets me work whenever I'm in town and available, he's great. I play on one of the mini-tours and I came in third place a while back and I bought the car with my earnings. It's the only money I've ever won. But my parents said it was okay, so I did it. I still live with them."

Mark and Niamh were very impressed with Sam. He was polite, very intelligent, and an excellent driver. They were each thinking *I hope we can have a child like Sam one day*. As they neared Greensboro, Niamh and Mark both dozed off, holding each other's hand. Sam didn't wake them until they pulled into the lot at Finnegan's. Eric and Amie came out to meet them and told Mark they'd arranged for a rental car for him, which was parked nearby. Then Eric said, "Ailen called and told us that you'd be staying at his wife's house here in town. We also made a hotel reservation for Niamh at the Kimpton."

Mark and Niamh were a bit confused by this statement, Mark asked, "A hotel reservation?"

"Yes, it's at the Kimpton, one of the best places in Winston. She'll love it, they have free wine from 6:00 to 7:00 each evening."

Then Niamh asked, "A hotel?"

"Yes, ma'am. It's not far from here."

"But I think I'll just stay with Mark over at the house, if that's okay." Eric and Amie both froze . . . literally froze. They didn't say anything, nor move a muscle. Niamh could easily see something was amiss, so she asked, "Are you okay? Is something wrong?"

Eric looked at Amie, then Amie looked at Niamh and said, "But you're not married yet."

Niamh asked, "What do you mean?"

"You're not married." Amie answered, "You can't stay in the same house if you're not married. Right?"

Mark and Niamh looked at each other, then Niamh nodded, and replied, "Of course, you're right, Amie. We weren't thinking. Thanks for arranging everything." Everyone then smiled, and Sam loaded the suitcases into Mark's rental car so he could take Niamh to the hotel. Mark told them that once he and Niamh got checked into their SEPARATE accommodations, they'd be back for dinner at Finnegan's so they could discuss the wedding arrangements for the following day.

Mark went in the hotel to make sure Niamh had no problems getting checked in, plus, he wanted to see the inside of the former R J Reynolds Tobacco building for himself. The building itself was the model for the Empire State Building in New York and at one time, the tallest building in North Carolina. Now, it was a first-class hotel that people from Winston-Salem would check-in and spend the night just because of its history as the former Reynolds Building. Mark was giddy as he walked around the lobby, then up the gilded elevator to Niamh's room. Once she unpacked her suitcase, they took the elevator to the very top of the building, where they could walk outside, like at the Empire State Building, and have a panoramic view of Winston-Salem.

Mark was as enraptured as a little boy at the spectacular views from the top. Niamh also enjoyed the scenery, especially towards the Blue Ridge Mountains, where Pilot Mountain dominated the view. However, she was happiest of all at the way it made Mark feel. She could sense the pride and enthusiasm that was bursting from him as he kept pointing out different scenes for her. After several minutes, when Mark slowed down enough, she put her arms around him and hugged him. He wanted that moment to last all evening. Niamh said, "Mark, I didn't know you felt so strongly about Winston-Salem. If it would make you happy, we could think about living here, if that's what you want."

Mark pulled back and looked directly in those enchanting emerald-green eyes and replied, "You would do that for me? Move here to Winston-Salem?"

"If it would make you happy, yes."

Mark kissed her, then hugged her again, and said, "Yes, I love Winston-Salem, and this hotel is special if you grew up here, like I did. But, as much as I love my hometown, I love you and Ireland and our life together much, much more. I could never get those rolling green hills out of my blood. The lakes, the mountains, the cliffs, the people . . . Niamh, I'm Irish now. I love America, especially North Carolina, but Ireland is in me—just as you are in me. I could never leave Ireland, just as I can never leave you. Don't you understand that?"

Niamh couldn't answer because she started crying uncontrollably. They lost concept of time for a while as they held each other tightly and thought of their lives and dreamed of their futures. Their revelry was broken when a busboy opened the door to the building and said, "Sorry to disturb y'all, but it's time for free wine down in the lobby. You wouldn't want to miss that."

No, they wouldn't. Niamh went back to the room to freshen up her makeup and Mark called Eric at Finnegan's and told him they'd be there in about an hour. The bar area inside the lobby was set up for the wine tasting each evening for all guests. It featured wines from the Yadkin Valley wine region. Tonight's specials featured wines from Piccione's, Raffaldini's, Laurel Gray, Jolo, Childress, Shelton, and Weathervane Wineries. A good mix of everything from dry to sweet, and all flavors in-between.

Mark's tastes ran toward the sweet wines of Childress and Weathervane, whereas Niamh liked the more, dry flavored wines from Piccione's and Raffaldini. The hour passed in a flash. Mark realized that after the tasting, with more Guinness to come at dinner, he'd better call a cab for the short ride over to the pub. Before they went inside, Mark stopped, and looked very seriously at Niamh, then asked, "Are you sure this is what you want to do? I mean ABSOLUTELY CERTAIN?"

"Mark, do you remember the first time we met, on the cliff?"

"Yes, of course I do."

"And do you remember what I told you about myself?"

Mark wasn't sure what she was referring to, but answered, "Yes, I remember everything."

"Then you'll know I am a descendant of the Sea Goddess, Tir-na- nOg. I have been waiting for this moment for over three-hundred years. I have been waiting for you for over three-hundred years. Nothing is going to stop us. Do you understand me, Mark? Nothing."

Now, Mark wanted to cry, but was brought back to the moment by Eric and Amie knocking on the window, waving for them to come inside and officially get the party started.

TWENTY-FIVE

THE PUB WAS CLOSED TO THE PUBLIC and decorated in a festive, celebratory fashion, with "Mark + Niamh" banners hung over the bar and seating area. There was no band, but Eric arranged for the speaker system to be tuned into one of the 24-hour radio stations that played popular music from Mark's era. Mark knew very few of the people there, and Niamh didn't know anyone, but they enjoyed it, nonetheless. Ailen's other employee in Winston-Salem, Desmond, came to the party with his wife Stella, both of whom were acquainted with Mark. All the other people there were friends of Eric and Amie, and they all brought wedding presents, which were being piled in the corner.

Mark was very surprised at all the gifts that were brought by people he'd never met, but he tried to thank as many as he could. The rest of the evening, he simply held Niamh's hand and enjoyed the moment; just as she did. After things had quieted down a bit, Eric and Amie, who had dyed her hair half-blonde and half-black, asked Mark and Amie to come back to the office with them to discuss something. They all entered the small office and Eric closed the door and said, "We have something to ask you that is very important to us. But it's okay if you say 'no,' we'll clearly understand, but we wanted to ask."

Mark answered, "Of course, Eric, ask away."

Eric took a deep breath, then looked over at Amie, and grabbed her hand before saying, "Would you let us get married with you at the church tomorrow? It would mean a great deal to us."

Mark didn't know how to respond. He was shocked. Niamh quickly said, "I thought you were already married."

Amie replied, "Well, technically and legally, we are. Our friend married us, but he only got ordained to do the ceremony. It wasn't in a church, and we want a marriage in a real church with a real minister, like you're having. And we would love to celebrate all this with you—if it's okay?"

Niamh looked over at Mark, then cried out, "Yes! It would be great! A day we'll all remember forever." Eric quickly ran outside and brought back four Guinness's for them to toast with. The girls started crying and hugging each other, while the guys shook hands and slapped each other on the back. They all returned to the party, announced it to the crowd, and invited them all to the ceremony at the church tomorrow. So much for Mark and Niamh's idea of a small, intimate wedding.

The party lasted until after midnight. The Guinness flowed, Blarney Burgers were served with sweet-potato fries or mac-and-cheese, and home-made cookies and ice cream were ready for anyone who wanted them. Mark never let go of Niamh's hand, exactly the way she wanted it. Finally, as everyone eventually left, Eric called Sam from the kitchen and asked him to drive Mark and Niamh back to their hotel and house. Eric's instructions to Sam were explicit: "Take Niamh back to the hotel, wait for Mark to come back out, then take him to his house." Mark thought, *I've waited three-hundred years, I can wait one more night.*

* * *

It was a beautiful day for a wedding. Niamh had brought her wedding ensemble with her: an off-white, slim-fitting, just below the knee, lovely, yet sexy-looking dress that she'd been saving for this day. Amie, on the other hand, had nothing in mind until she woke up in the morning. She looked through her closet and couldn't decide what to choose. She called her best friend, Susan, to come over and help her decide. Susan, instead, brought something with her that Amie fell in love with-- a sheer black top with a matching black, mini-skirt that was much too short for her to sit down in. It could only be worn standing up. Amie already had a pair of knee-high black boots that perfectly matched the ensemble.

Mark had brought the only suit he owned, which was charcoal gray, and a little wrinkled from the flight. Eric had rented the most expensive tuxedo in the shop, and had it quickly altered to fit his trim body. Unfortunately, no one had told Opie, the preacher, that it was going to be such a formal affair. He assumed he was just going to perform a quick, informal ceremony for two out-of-towners. That's why he showed up at the church wearing cargo pants, a ban-lon shirt, and loafers with no socks. It didn't matter. All eyes were on the two brides.

Niamh was as radiant as the sun shining through on Easter morning. Amie was resiliently dressed head-to-toe in black, with her hair parted down the middle, black on one side and blonde on the other. Never in the history of weddings has there been two more beautiful, glorious, elegant, and flawless looking brides— at least, that's what Mark and Eric thought.

Niamh kept waiting for something to happen. She was nearly convinced that leprechauns would find some way to prevent her wedding again. They didn't. Eric was about to burst with pride and anticipation as he saw the love of his life standing before him. They would NOT be sleeping in separate abodes tonight. Opie did a fantastic job with the dual ceremony and when he finally got to the final sentence and pronounced both couples, man-and-wife, till death do them part, the church erupted with joy. Someone had brought a confetti gun into the church (obviously not a Moravian) and when each husband kissed his bride, confetti shot up into the air and rained down upon everyone in attendance. Mark thought *wow, this is amazing. After everything that has happened, Niamh and I are* finally *together.* Eric thought, *I can't believe it. Tonight's the night!* And Opie thought, *I sure hope someone cleans this mess up before the Deacons see it.*

They used the church's reception room for the party afterwards—no alcohol involved. After last night, no one complained. After each couple had received all the congratulations from everyone, Mark asked Eric what he and Amie were going to for their honeymoon. "Tonight, we'll just enjoy being with each other, Mark. That's enough."

"But where are you going?"

"We aren't going anywhere but back to work in the morning."

Mark was shocked, "No! You must go somewhere to celebrate."

Eric answered, "No, we're good. This is all we've ever wanted and now we have it. Plus, we have no one to run the pub."

Mark said, "I'll run the pub. You two take off, enjoy yourselves."

Eric grinned and added, "Oh, we'll enjoy ourselves tonight. Don't worry about us. We're fine. Where are you and Niamh going?"

Mark hadn't even thought about that question. Everything had happened so fast that they never discussed a honeymoon. He didn't answer Eric's question, he turned and found Niamh talking with several of Amie's friends and pulled her away. "What are we going to do for our honeymoon?"

"We're going back home. Our home. To Ireland, to our daughter, to our friends, to our life."

And that settled it.

Eric and Amie went back to her place to consummate their marriage and spend the night together as husband and wife. Mark took Niamh back to the hotel for their first night as husband and wife. After a complimentary glass of champagne, they went up to the roof of the hotel again. It was a clear, bright night, with hundreds of thousands of stars twinkling in the distance, celebrating this grand occasion. Since it was well after midnight, there were no other guests with them. They had the entire deck to themselves.

They star-gazed and gazed into each other's eyes as well. It was a dream come true for each of them. Niamh took Mark's hand and led him to the west side of the building where they stopped and Niamh said, "Out there are the cliffs of the Irish coast, Mark. The rugged coastline, with dozens of little islands sparkling in the mist." They both stared off into the void and dreamed of that vision. Then she led him to the south side and continued, "Imagine the great cities of Galway and Killarney and the peninsulas of Dingle and Kerry, Mark. Lands so great and beautiful that words have yet to be formed that can describe them." Mark, again, stared off into the vastness, and could almost envision the green-coated landscapes Niamh described.

Then she led him to the east side of the building where she said, "And out there, Mark, are the castles and ruins, thousands of years old, that our ancestors built and protected. Out there is the heartland of Ireland—Dublin, Crough Patrick, the Rock of Cashel, and all the other monuments of our existence. Do you see it, Mark?"

"Yes, I do see it."

Then, she led him to the north side of the building and hugged him tightly while they both stared off into the eternity of dreams, and said, "And out there, Mark, is our home. The place where I've been waiting for you to come into my life and my existence for over three-hundred years. It's where we'll raise our family. It's where our love will grow and it's where we will thrive and plant the seeds of our future together. It's where we are, Mark. Do you see that as well?"

He held her tightly and answered, "I've always seen it. It's been in my mind for the entirety of my being. You are my existence, Niamh. Without you, I don't exist. You are my life." Eventually, they made their way back to Niamh's room, their room now. Niamh drew a hot bath in the over-sized tub, while Mark lit candles he had brought with him on the sink, counter, and floor. She poured some type of bubbly mix into the water, got in first, and dipped under the water. When Mark entered the bathroom, all he could see was her beautiful light-brown hair, tinged with red, and the most gorgeous green eyes he had ever imagined, but he also knew what lay under those bubbles.

He brought them each a glass of champagne and then he climbed into the tub as well. The champagne was nice, but it was totally unnecessary. No drink, nor drug, nor dream could make them feel as good as they felt right now. It may have taken three-hundred years for them to come together . . . but it was worth the wait.

TWENTY-SIX

THE MORNING AFTER THE WEDDING, Mark and Niamh ordered room service and had breakfast in bed. It was so good that they discussed having lunch in bed as well. Then Mark's phone rang. It was Eric. He said, "Mark, I'm so sorry, we'll be there in no time. I'm so, so sorry. This will never happen again."

Mark interrupted him and asked, "Whoa, Eric. Sorry about what? What's wrong?"

"We sort of . . . umm . . . overslept; yeah, that's it, we overslept. We're dressing now and . . . I didn't mean we were undressed, Mark, it's just that we're . . . umm."

"Eric, slow down. Everything is alright. Take your time. In fact, why don't you two take off this morning and come in around noon. I'll let everyone know."

"Oh, no, Mark! We could never do that. We'll by right over. We've finished up here and we'll be on our way in a flash."

Mark, still having a little southern, redneck in him, asked, "You just finished up what, Eric?"

Silence. Then Eric said, "We've just finished up, you know, umm, things around here."

Mark was loving it now, "No, I don't know. What things?"

More silence. Then Amie's voice came on the phone, and she said, "I'm so sorry, Mark. It'll never happen again. We'll be on our way in five minutes." Before Mark could tell her to take off the entire morning, she disconnected the call. Mark tried to call them back, but they didn't answer. Oh, well, since Eric and Amie were going down to the pub, Niamh convinced Mark to follow through on their plans and indeed have lunch in bed, if that's what it could be called.

After "lunch-in-bed" they made several calls, starting with Niamh's daughter back in Ireland. They also spoke with Niamh's parents, who wanted to speak to Mark and congratulate him as well. Then Mark called Ailen to thank him for everything and assure him things would be back to normal very soon. Ailen said, "I hope not."

Mark didn't understand, he asked, "What? Why?"

"Because Mark. You're married now. Your top priority is Niamh and taking care of your family. Everything else is secondary. The businesses will be fine. Do you understand me, son?" That really wasn't a question. It was more of a command from Ailen to Mark. He then asked Mark, "When do you want me to make flight arrangements for you? Are you staying for a while in Winston-Salem?"

"Ailen, this might sound a little strange to you, but we want to get back home as soon as possible."

Ailen asked, "So, Ireland is 'home' to you now?"

"It has been for quite some time. You know that."

"Aye, I'll make plans for the next flight out. I'll call you back."

* * *

There were no open seats available until the following day. Which meant Mark and Niamh now had all day and evening to enjoy themselves. Since they'd already had "breakfast in bed" and "lunch in bed," they decided to give Eric and Amie a present on their honeymoon. They went to Finnegan's and found them both hard at work. One thing was different however, Amie had dyed her hair back to purple, and she had a new, small tattoo on her shoulder, which was a heart with their names written inside it. When Mark walked up to the bar area, Eric quickly came over and started apologizing for being late this morning.

Niamh said, "You should have stayed out all day. It's your honeymoon!"

"Oh, no," Eric said, "we told Mark he could always count on us, no matter what, and we meant it."

Just then Amie walked up. Mark looked at them both and said, "Get out. Go somewhere—go nowhere—but get out of here and have some fun."

"But . . ." Eric tried to argue.

"I said, GET OUT, and I mean it. I'm your boss and I'm ordering you out. But come back by noon tomorrow, we have to be in Raleigh to catch a flight."

Amie tried to say something, but Niamh said, "Out!" They both smiled and took their aprons off, and Eric looked at Mark when again Niamh said, "Out, now!" When the couple left, Niamh looked over at Mark and added, "How many people can say they actually ran a pub on their honeymoon?"

Everything went smoothly, except for a couple of times when Niamh got confused with nickels, quarters, and dimes—she was used to Euros. Other than that, things went smoothly on the first day of the rest of their lives.

* * *

Ailen had gotten their tickets, and Eric had arranged for Sam to drive them to the airport in Raleigh again. There was a little bit of sadness for Mark as he left his hometown once again . . . he still loved Winston-Salem. After they were on the road, Niamh asked Sam about his golf future, and what his plans were. He replied, "Well, I'm going to play as much as possible. It's an expensive sport, with all the travel, lodging, and food. I'll do it as long as I can. I do love it very much. There are a few small events in Ireland, England, and Scotland coming up. Not sure I can afford to go over there, however. That's very expensive."

Niamh said, "Look, if there's a tournament anywhere in the northern part of Ireland, you can stay with us and save yourself a lot of money. Anytime at all, just let us know, okay?"

"Yes, ma'am. That's very nice. I'll take a look at the schedule and see what's coming up." The rest of the conversations were all "Yes, ma'ams and yes, sirs" from Sam. He was a very polite young man. He dropped them off in front of the terminal and helped them carry their luggage inside. Then Mark shook his hand and Niamh gave him a hug and a hundred dollars in twenty-dollar bills. It was unclear which one of these Sam enjoyed more.

The flight left as scheduled and Mark and Niamh held hands and dozed through much of it. When it was obvious that the airplane was slowing down and losing altitude, Niamh raised her window and looked out, only to see a thick cloud cover as they came near the coast of Ireland. It was early morning in Ireland and the sun had just risen, but nothing was visible but a thick layer of clouds. She woke Mark and said, "Look, we're almost home. Isn't it beautiful?"

Mark leaned over and looked out the window and replied, "Yes, it is, almost as beautiful as you." They held hands tightly as the airplane rolled down the runway at Shannon. There was a light mist falling but isn't that expected here in the land of leprechauns, clover, Guinness, and love?

Yes.

* * *

Ailen had pre-arranged for a rental car to be ready for them. When they got their bags and went through customs, they made their way to the Hertz office and filled out the paperwork. When Mark finished, the Hertz lady thanked him and gave him an envelope addressed to "Mark and Niamh." He showed it to Niamh, and she opened it. It read, "To the happy couple, glad to have you back home. This is confirmation of a three-day stay in Galway at the Skellig Hotel. From all your friends in Dungloe:

Ailen and Gabriella

Eileen and all the staff

Claire and all the girls and cooks

GC and Layla"

The Skellig Hotel was a first-class hotel in Galway, located on Galway Bay, with fantastic views in all directions. When they finally got into the rental car, Mark called Ailen to thank him, but he didn't answer, so he called Eileen to thank her, and she didn't answer either. Claire answered. "Hello, Mark."

"Claire, I wanted to call and thank you and the others for the generous gift you gave us."

"So, you're definitely married now. Is that right?"

"Yes, finally."

"Does that mean you won't be trying to visually undress me anymore?"

"Claire!"

"Well, I just wanted to know. A girl needs to know how things like this stand."

"Things like what? There never was anything standing in the first place."

"Well, if I remember correctly, and I think I do, you did kiss me one night at a dance. Did you not?"

Mark didn't know whether to hang up, cuss her, or keep trying to argue—which is what she would have wanted. So, he said, "Thanks again, Claire. And please tell all the others, thanks as well."

A moment of silence, then Claire responded, "You do know that I'm at home right now, just getting out of the shower."

Mark screamed, "Claire!"

She laughed and said, "Goodbye, Mark, have fun . . . that is, if you know how." She disconnected the call before he could respond.

TWENTY-SEVEN

GALWAY CITY WAS FANTASTIC. They walked hand-in-hand down the Salthill promenade along the coast and listened to musicians play guitars, fiddles, accordions, and harps. The sights, sounds, and memories of Galway would live in their hearts forever. They stopped for scones and tea (coffee for Mark), then sat on a bench and watched the waves crash into the coast as they dreamed of what they had and what they wanted, which were both the same.

The following morning, Niamh convinced Mark to take the boat ride out to the Aran Islands, several miles offshore in Galway Bay. The islands hold an unusual number of sacred and historical sites, of which Dun Aonghasa is the most prominent. The remains of this fort sit on a cliff three-hundred feet above the ocean and have been there for over three-thousand years. There were several small boats that ferried tourists out to Inis Mor, the main island of the group, where Dun Aonghasa was located. What neither Niamh nor Mark realized was how rough the seas were between Galway and Inis Mor.

The twenty-passenger boat they were on had no chance against the Irish sea. The boat was at the mercy of the waves, and it lost the fight. The bow of the boat would point up toward the sky as it faced the incoming waves, then would point down into the ocean as it passed the wave. Up and down, side to side—the thirty-minute ride seemed to last thirty hours for the newlyweds.

When they finally reached the shore and exited the boat, they almost made it to the restrooms . . . unfortunately, they didn't. Mark fell victim first, and when Niamh saw him upheaving his breakfast, she immediately joined him. Not only depositing their breakfast off the pathway, but also everything they had eaten since their first meal in Finnegan's Wake, several days earlier.

They were so violent in their upheavals that when their bodies were finally completely empty, they only then noticed that their clothes were completely soiled as well. They saw a tourist shop nearby with some benches outside. Mark sat down and leaned against the wall while Niamh went into the shop to buy them new clothes. The tourist clothes were meant to be souvenirs of the trip and were fashioned after the Irish culture of a thousand years ago—but they fit well enough. They each changed clothes in the restrooms and then threw their old clothes into the trash bins.

After twenty minutes or so, the effects of the boat ride began to dissipate. Then they started on the thirty-minutes hike up the hill to the cliffs of Dun Aonghasa. It was not an easy walk. They stopped several times to sit on the rock walls that bordered the trail. Niamh didn't want to get her "new" clothes dirty by sitting on the wall. Mark didn't care. They eventually arrived at the cliffs and almost instantly their nausea left them as the wonder and excitement of the moment overcame them. They sat on the rocky wall of the old fort and stared out into the vastness, never releasing the tight grip of each other's hand. The sea was over three-hundred feet straight down and over three-thousand miles across.

They took pictures of each other and had other tourists take pictures of them together in their newlywed costumes of ancient Ireland. It was a grand afternoon, until they realized they had to get back on the small boat for the ride back to Galway. At least there was nothing inside their bodies left to throw up. Now it would only be enduring the rolling waves and rocky motions of the small boat. As they made their way back to the pier, they noticed several advertising signs posted on the walkway. One of which read, "Airboats to Dun Aonghasa."

Mark grabbed a pamphlet and they both read it, "Airboats to and from Dun Aonghasa, leaving Galway every hour. Ride a foot or two above the seas on this smooth and comfortable journey." They couldn't believe what they were reading. They immediately headed down the pier to the office of the airboats. The attendant assured them the ride would be as smooth as riding down the freeway. He was right. The ride was so smooth, they had a cup of coffee and tea as they tried their best to forget the unforgettable ride over.

* * *

The remainder of their stay in Galway was unforgettable and unmentionable to most friends and all family members. On the drive home they stopped in Donegal, where Niamh lived for a while after the fateful first meeting with Mark. They drove by her old home, located on Sky Road, an apt name for this small, rolling passage that overlooked Donegal Bay. Out in the bay were dozens of small islands that one could stare at and dream illusory thoughts, which is exactly what Niamh did in those days. They pulled off the road across the street from her old home and leaned against the car as they once more stared off into a dreamland of hopes and wonders.

They finally made it back home just before dark and spent the rest of the evening with Ennis, Niamh's daughter. It was a dream come true for all three of them. In the morning, Mark had to get back to work and check on the businesses in town. From his phone calls while he was away, he was pretty sure things were running very smoothly. He was wrong. His first stop was the local feed and grain store that almost never had any problems. The manager of the store was an elderly man named Guarino, who had been running the store longer than anyone could remember.

Mark walked in and Guarino and two other elderly men congratulated him on his marriage. It took Mark about three seconds to notice that several shelves were nearly empty. As he looked around at the bare surroundings, Guarino said, "Hey, Mark, listen to this joke, *A young lad said to his grandfather, 'Make a frog noise for me, Grandad.'*

'No, son, I don't feel like making a frog noise right now.'

'Oh, please, Grandad, make a frog noise.'

'No, I don't want to.'

'Oh, please, Grandad, make a frog noise.'

'Why is it so important to you that I make a frog noise?'

'Mum says that when you croak, we can have this house.'

The other old men all laughed and slapped Guarino on the back while Mark continued to stare at the empty shelves. When everyone calmed down, Mark asked, "Why are the shelves empty, Guarino?"

"Because you weren't here to order anything."

"Guarino, you know how to order supplies. You don't need me to do that."

"But you have the checkbook. I can't pay for supplies. Plus, ordering things is your job, isn't it?" When he asked this question, the other old men all turned to look at Mark to see what his answer was going to be. Mark knew what he wanted to say to Guarino, that was the easy part. Then, he thought, *I'm so lucky they can't hear what I'm thinking.* So, he smiled, told Guarino to order all the supplies he needed and send him the bills, then he shook hands with everyone, and headed for his next stop.

Everything seemed very normal and quiet in the bar. The bartender was drawing some drafts for three customers and a couple of waitresses were taking orders. Mark didn't see Eileen anywhere, so he walked back toward the office and knocked on the door. He heard a voice saying, "Hello, c'mon in, Mark." When he walked in, she said, "We're fully stocked here. You can leave if you want."

He wanted to say, *I'll leave when I'm ready.* And, *How did you know it was me?* And, *Why would you say you're fully stocked?* But he didn't. He knew Eileen but didn't know how she knew things like that. Instead, he said, "Good afternoon, Eileen. Anything I can do to help?"

She didn't even look up from her desk and replied, "No, we're fine." Mark wanted to say something else. He wanted to have a conversation with her, but she never looked up from her paperwork. After a few awkward moments, he said,

"Okay, see you later." As he walked through the pub, he asked the bartender and one of the waitresses if anything was wrong with Eileen. They both agreed that she seemed fine, maybe a little quiet, but fine.

Next stop was the restaurant and Claire. She was also in the back office, busy with some billings. When he opened the door, she seemed a bit startled, and said, "Mark! I didn't know you were here. Why didn't you call?"

Instead of answering that question, he asked, "Have you spoken with Eileen lately? She seems a little bothered by something. Is she okay?"

Claire sternly replied, "No, she's not okay!"

"Well, what's wrong with her?"

Claire walked over and shut the door behind Mark and said, "Because she likes you, dumbo, I told you that."

"What do you mean, she likes me?"

"She LIKES you! She always has. I told you that, but just like forever, you don't pay any attention to what I say."

Mark took a few seconds, then asked, "She likes me as in HOW?"

Claire shook her head and said, "As in she wants to jump your bones, you blind, dumb man!"

"What?"

"How can you be so stupid, Mark? She's always wanted you since she's been here, but she has always known you had Niamh in your head and heart, so she never said anything or did anything."

Mark asked, "Are you sure? She's never said anything to me."

"Of course, I'm sure, Mark. I don't how you can be so blind."

"But . . ."

"Let it go. She will never say anything or do anything, I can promise you that. She likes Niamh too much to ever get in the way. She just can't help feeling like she does. Lord knows I don't know why!" Mark didn't know what to say, or how to feel. Claire continued, "Go on home to your wife. Eileen will be fine. She's too professional to ever let her feelings get in the way of anything. Just go home and pretend like you never knew any of this." He started to go back to the pub and talk with Eileen, but what would he say?

TWENTY-EIGhT

THE FOLLOWING COUPLE OF WEEKS found things back to their old ways. Ennis was back in school. Niamh was setting up the household. Ailen was travelling somewhere-- no one knew where. Claire was in top-notch form, Jims was the friend Mark always needed, and Eileen was . . . quiet. Mark had even arranged for Siobhan's little band to play at his pub after she finished playing at Jim's pub. Might as well make all the men in Dungloe as happy as those in Burtonport.

But Eileen was quiet. She was never the talkative one, the loud one, or the bossy one—she was just Eileen—the one that everybody liked and trusted. But Mark had noticed a change, ever since he and Niamh returned as a married couple. There was no longer any coffee waiting for him in the pub when he arrived each morning. No one else noticed these small changes, except Mark. He noticed them. Then, one morning, after he had stopped by the restaurant and argued with Claire, he walked in the pub and there was a pot of coffee brewing and an empty cup on the bar where he usually sat.

Mark smiled and thought, *great, things are getting back to normal.* Then the bartender came from the back room and spotted Mark and came walking toward him carrying an envelope. He was usually a happy young man, but not today. Mark thought someone must have died in his family, it looked as though he might start crying. He handed Mark the envelope without saying a word, then stood back as he watched Mark open it. It read,

Mark, I hate to do this to you, but I must resign immediately. I have a family emergency that requires my attention, and I must leave now. I appreciate all you've done for me, and I apologize for leaving so suddenly, but I have no choice. I hope you understand. I won't be coming back and please don't try to contact me.

Good luck to you and your family,

Eileen

Mark was stunned. Then he thought, *this must be a joke*. He looked around the pub hoping to see Eileen and the others laughing at this practical joke. He didn't see anyone but the sad bartender, now sitting at a table sipping a Guinness at 9:15 in the morning. He walked over and sat down across the table from him and said, "Warren, did you know about this?"

"Not until this morning, boss. She told me she was leaving and told me to hand this note to you."

"What did she say?"

Warren took a big gulp from his pint and answered, "She told me she had to leave, that I'd be fine, and not to worry about anything. Then I asked her why she had to leave but she didn't answer, she just gave me the envelope and told me to give it to you. Then she told me to brew you a pot of coffee, and she walked out the door. I saw her get in her car and noticed that it was packed with all sorts of stuff."

Mark quickly walked up the stairs to the apartment above the pub where Eileen lived. The door was closed but unlocked. Mark opened it and found it empty except for the furniture. All of Eileen's personal belongings were gone and the closets were empty . . . she was indeed gone. Mark sat on the couch and reread the note. It still didn't make any sense. Why would she leave like this? Where did she go? He didn't know where this "family" she mentioned even lived. In fact, he knew very little of Eileen's personal life. He knew she moved to Dungloe from somewhere in the south of Ireland, but he didn't know where.

He first called Niamh and told her what had happened and asked if Eileen had mentioned anything to her. She had not. Niamh was just as shocked as Mark. He went back downstairs and waited for the remainder of the staff to start coming in so he could question them. Eventually, he learned that no one had any clue of why Eileen had left so suddenly. He knew that Eileen and Claire were somewhat friendly, so he walked down the street to the restaurant. Claire was at the cash register with a customer. He waited for her to finish, then motioned her back to the office.

When she walked in, he closed the door and Claire said, "No, Mark, you're married now!" When Mark didn't react, she asked, "What's wrong?"

"Eileen's gone."

"What do you mean, she's gone? Gone where?"

"She left the pub. She left Dungloe. She left us all. She only left this note that says she won't be coming back."

For once in her life, Claire was silent. They both stood there staring at each other, neither knowing what to say. Then, Claire said, "I should have seen it coming. I should have known."

Mark anxiously asked, "Known what?"

"Known that she couldn't live here knowing that you were now married. I told you before she wanted you, Mark. She probably couldn't take it every day, seeing you come in the pub all happy and satisfied, while her heart was broken. She just couldn't take that misery, so she left. It's all I can think of."

Mark was silent for a few seconds, then said, "I don't know if I believe that. I think I would have known if Eileen had a thing for me. She never said or did anything for me to think that she did. I think you're fantasizing all this, Claire."

Claire abruptly walked out of the office and yelled, "Come here!" Immediately, her staff all came walking back to the office. When they had all assembled, Claire said, "I'm going to ask you all a question and I expect an honest answer, is that understood?" They all nodded, then Claire asked, "As far as you each know, did Eileen have a thing for Mark? A crush, or something like that?"

She pointed at Randy who answered, "Yes, ma'am, of course she did."

She then pointed at Shirley who said, "Of course, everyone knew that, ma'am."

Then, Kay, who nodded a little and looked over at Mark, and said, "Yes, she loved you, sir."

Before Claire could ask the dishwasher and the busboy, Mark walked out the door. He didn't know where to go, but he had to go somewhere. Then he thought of the pub. Without Eileen there, it was without a manager, he had to go back and sort things out. When he walked in the door to the pub, the bartender was still sipping on a Guinness, maybe his second one, or third, Mark didn't know. The cook saw Mark and walked over to him asking all sorts of questions, that he had no clue how to answer. Then, a couple of waitresses came to him asking about their schedules and when they were to work and be off. Mark was completely overwhelmed.

He told them all that everything would be okay. He'd answer all their questions in a few minutes, but first he had to clear up some details. He went back into the office, shut the door, and called Niamh, saying, "What am I going to do?"

Naimh answered, "I'll be right there. Don't worry, we'll figure it out." She grabbed some stuff and made it to the pub in about twenty minutes. Mark was still in the office with the door shut. Before she could get to the door, the cook, the waitresses, and the busboy were all asking her the same questions they'd asked Mark. Niamh answered every question and got them back to their duties. She didn't know if her answers were accurate, but at least everyone was back at work.

When she walked in the office, Mark was sitting at the desk with Eileen's note still in his hand. She took the note and read it, then said, "We'll get through this, Mark. Don't worry." He never replied. He only looked at her and smiled. He knew that with her by his side, he could do anything. He didn't know how he'd do it, but he knew they would. She brought him a cup of coffee and made herself a cup of tea as they sat and discussed things. It was still hard to fathom that Eileen was gone.

After an hour or so, Mark decided to call his friend Jims, who also ran and operated a pub over in Burtonport. Mark told him what had happened and asked for some advice, Jims said, "Well, son, you've got to hire a manager right now. And I mean RIGHT NOW, son!"

"I know that Jims, I just don't know anyone. Do you?"

Jims was silent for a few seconds, but then said, "I do, Mark, but I don't know if you will like my suggestion."

"Tell me. I'm desperate here, Jims."

"Siobhan. She'd be great. You'll love her."

"Siobhan? I don't need a singer, Jims. I need a bar manager."

"I know that knucklehead. That's what Siobhan does. The singing gig is just a sideline for her. She runs a small pub over in Clifden. She'd love to take a step up and manage a nice pub like yours."

Mark told Jims he'd call him back and then started thinking, *Siobhan? Could she do this?* His thoughts were interrupted by Niamh's cell phone ringing. It was the school. Ennis was feeling sick, and Niamh had to go pick her up. As soon as she left, the questions from the staff started again: from the cook, the waitresses, the bartender . . . from everyone. Mark told them to wait, that he'd be right out. Then he called Jims back and asked him to call Siobhan and see if she was interested. He sure hoped she would be.

TWENTY-NINE

JIMS CONTACTED SIOBHAN ABOUT THE JOB, and she agreed to come over and speak with Mark. Every time Mark had ever seen Siobhan, including the times she was with her band, and the few times they "dated," she had always worn a very short skirt, which was appropriate for a woman of her shape and beauty. Not this time. She came dressed in a pantsuit, and looked very professional as she walked into the pub. She already looked like the boss and Mark hadn't even hired her yet. He offered her something to drink and she declined, and said, "Look Mark, I know we have a social history together, but this is different. If I'm going to work here, for you, I must know that it's strictly business, and our relationship will be nothing but professional."

"Of course, Siobhan, that's the only way it can work. Plus, you know that Niamh and I are married now, right?"

"Married?"

"Yes, I thought JIms may have told you."

"No, Mark, I didn't know that. I'm very happy for you. That makes a world of difference to me. I mean, I didn't want this job to be some sort of way for you to . . . well, never mind. I'm just glad to hear that." Mark smiled but didn't reply, then Siobhan added, "So I can wear my usual clothes, or is there any dress code here?"

"No, you can wear whatever you please, as long as it's appropriate for work." She smiled and then they discussed what Mark expected from her as manager of the pub, what the hours were, and what the salary would be. Siobhan had a few questions, but everything was easy for them both to agree on. Mark took her into the pub and introduced her to everyone, then they sat at a table in the corner while he called Niamh to come down and meet Siobhan. Niamh had seen her band play but had never spoken to her before.

After the meeting with Niamh, Mark took Siobhan down the street to introduce her to Claire. This meeting didn't go as well as Mark was hoping. When they walked in, Claire was busy cleaning off a table, and never looked up to see Mark. He said, "Claire, sorry to interrupt you, but I'd like you to meet our new pub manager."

Claire never looked up from the table and replied, "Nice to meet you, sir, but I'm busy right now, in case you can't tell."

Before Mark could say anything, Siobhan answered, "Nice to meet you as well, but I'm not a sir, miss."

Upon hearing this, Claire, stopped and looked up at Siobhan, then looked at Mark and said, "I thought you were hiring a man."

"I never said I was hiring a man."

Claire looked back at Siobhan, then replied, "And she's going to manage the pub? Really?"

"Claire, that's very inappropriate."

"Oh, I get it now. She's the hussy you were shagging before Niamh. Makes perfect sense now."

"Claire!" Before any more words could be uttered, Claire dropped her dishes back on the table, turned, and walked away. Siobhan said,

"It's okay, Mark. Let it go."

"No, I won't let it go. Stay here, I'll be right back." Mark followed Claire back to the office and shut the door as he stared at her. He was fuming and didn't know where to start.

Claire said, "What? What do you want? I'm busy here."

"Claire, I can't believe you were so rude out there. What was that all about? You don't even know her! I expect you to go back out there and apologize to her right now."

"I won't do it. I won't apologize to that hussy. You can fire me if you want to, but I won't apologize to that boyfriend-stealing-witch." Now, it started to make a little sense to Mark. He asked,

"What do you mean by that?"

"You heard me! She's a witch and I will never be friends with her."

"I'm not asking you to be friends with her. I was just introducing her to you. I didn't know you two knew each other."

"Well, we do!"

Mark looked at her and asked, "Well?"

"She went behind my back and stole my boyfriend last year. She's a hussy and a witch and I'll never be friends with her, Mark."

"Okay, I understand. We're going to leave for now. Just calm down and everything will be okay."

"It won't be okay if you expect me to work with her!"

"You don't have to work with her, Claire. She'll be running the pub and you're running the restaurant, and never shall your paths meet . . . unless I need you two to do something for me. Then, I'll expect you both to act professionally and courteous to each other. Do you understand?" Silence. After about thirty seconds, Mark asked a bit more forcefully, "Do you understand, Claire?" This time she nodded slightly and said,

"Now if you don't mind, I have to get back to work. One of the girls called in sick today." Mark walked back out, but Siobhan had gone outside to wait for him. They walked down the street a bit and found a bench to sit on, and Mark asked her,

"So, you and Claire know each other?"

"Not exactly. About a year ago, my band was playing at a pub and during the intermission, this guy, whom I'd never met before, came up to me and started talking. He seemed nice and friendly and asked if I'd like to have a drink with him sometime. I told him that would be nice and gave him my phone number to call me later. That's it. He never called me, but she did."

"Claire? She called you?"

"Oh yeah, and it wasn't nice. When I answered my phone she started with the boyfriend-stealing- witch junk, then started calling me all sorts of names and making wild insinuations about me and her boyfriend shacking up and all kinds of weird stuff. She's a nut case, Mark."

Mark asked, "Had you ever met Claire face-to-face before today?"

"Only once. She came to a pub where my band was playing one night and walked up to the stage and cussed me out. Then she turned to the audience and told everyone I was a boyfriend-stealing-slut. Then she walked out, and I've never seen her since, until today."

"Did you start dating the boyfriend?"

"Heavens no! I never saw him again either." They both sat there for a minute or two, until a light rain started coming down. Then they got up and walked back to the pub. When they went back to the office, Siobhan asked, "So, do I still have the job, or not?"

Mark smiled and answered, "Of course you do. Welcome to our world, Siobhan."

She also smiled and asked, "What world is that?"

"The world where Claire hates everyone. You're one of us now."

* * *

Mark showed Siobhan the vacant apartment upstairs and told her she could have it if she wanted. It was agreed that Siobhan would start work in two weeks, after giving her notice at her current pub. When she left, Mark's phone rang. It was Ailen. He said, "So I hear you've hired some boyfriend-stealing-slut as the new manager." Then he started laughing as Mark said,

"Didn't take Claire long to call and complain, did it?"

"No, it didn't. I met Siobhan once, very attractive lady. Does she have what you're looking for in a manager?"

"Yeah, Ailen, she'll be good. Sorry that Claire bothered you with this. What did you tell her?"

"I told her that if she ever went behind your back again and called me, that it would be the last phone call she'd ever make working for us." Mark smiled, then asked,

"Thanks, Ailen. By the way, where are you and Gabriella now?"

"You don't want to know, son. Trust me." And with that reply, Ailen disconnected the call.

TḢIRTY

IT TOOK SIOBHAN LESS THAN TWO DAYS to feel comfortable in her new job and not require Mark's help any longer. And, she began wearing her favorite skirts, which greatly increased the sale of Guinness in the pub. One afternoon when Mark was in the back storeroom of the pub taking inventory, Claire walked in unannounced. Mark wondered why she would leave the restaurant in the middle of the day, but he soon found out. "Mark, we need to talk."

"Okay . . . talk."

"It's about your new bar manager."

Mark knew this conversation would be coming soon. "What about her?"

"It's about the way she dresses, Mark. Or, should I say, the way she doesn't dress!"

"What's wrong with the way she dresses? It seems that all our customers love the way she dresses."

"That's the problem, Mark! She's dressing like a tramp. Like a . . . you know what I mean."

"It's a free country, Claire. A person can dress however they like, if it's professional and not in bad taste."

"That's the problem, Mark, it is in bad taste. Very bad taste if you ask me."

"I don't remember anyone asking you, Claire. Plus, I've had no complaints from our customers."

"Well how would you like it if I started dressing like that? What would you say then?"

Mark smiled and asked, "Are you going to start wearing short skirts, Claire?"

"I might!"

"If it makes you happy, then go right ahead. Your customers might enjoy the change."

She took a step closer to Mark and asked, "What do you mean by that?"

"I don't mean anything."

"Are you saying they don't like the way I dress now?"

"I never said anything, Claire."

She took one step closer to Mark, then uttered, "Hmmph!" With that said, she turned and walked out the door. A minute or two later, Siobhan walked in and asked,

"What was that about?"

"Nothing. Just Claire being Claire."

"I know she doesn't like me, Mark, but I hope it's not causing any trouble."

"Don't worry about her. She'll be fine. She always needs to have something to complain about."

Siobhan went back out to help with the bustling pub business. Mark picked up his phone and called Niamh for two reasons:

first, he loved hearing her voice, and second, to fill her in on the latest Claire episode. Even though they'd been married for quite some time now, Mark still felt a sense of joy and surprise each evening when he opened the door to their house and Niamh was there. It was almost like magic, and his sense of wonder that his dream had been fulfilled was never ending.

* * *

As was usual with Claire, she settled down after a few days. Everyone thought she might start wearing miniskirts, like Siobhan, just to prove a point, but she didn't. She stuck to her usual ankle length Amish dress, no makeup whatsoever, and her hair tied tightly in a bun on top of her head. That was Claire. Siobhan had the market on short skirts and none of the men in town had any complaints. But more importantly, she ran the pub without a hitch. Business was great. The staff seemed competent and satisfied, with no issues, which was hard to do in a small town where everyone knew everyone else.

Niamh spent her mornings getting Ennis ready for school, then cleaning the house and preparing meals. She would do her shopping, read a little, while she sat on the sofa with hot cup of tea, and stared absently out into the bay, where several small islands were scattered about. She was in love with her life. Usually, she would go into town and meet Mark for lunch, or just to talk. They would sit at a table in the pub and hold hands like two teenagers out on their first date. No one would admit it, but all the townspeople were jealous of what Mark and Niamh had . . . it was special.

One Thursday morning, Mark received a call from Ailen, whom he hadn't heard from in several weeks. He was in Winston-Salem, not to check on Finnegan's Wake, which was doing very well, but he and the beautiful Gabriella were there visiting her family and friends. Ailen had come to really appreciate Winston and the culture and loved visiting there for extended stays. After the initial "hello's" and "how are you's" Ailen came to the point of the phone call. He said, "I have become aware of an interesting business proposition here in Winston and I wanted to get your thoughts, since you grew up here."

Mark replied, "Okay, what is it?"

"There's a brewery on the market, just down the street from Finnegan's, and it looks very interesting. From what I've heard, the two owners of the place have decided to cash in their profits and start travelling the world before they get too old. Can't say that I blame them, but the brewery looks like a nice opportunity. I've had Desmond look into it and he thinks it's a gold mine." Mark knew a lot of the businesses in Winston and asked Ailen which brewery he was interested in. "Fiddlin' Fish." Ailen replied.

Mark knew it well. He enjoyed going there when he lived in Winston. Ailen continued, "You know they do their own craft beers, which are all great, by the way, but I was thinking of adding Guinness and a couple of other Irish beers to the mix. What do you think?"

"It sounds like a great opportunity, Ailen. Have you researched it all, looked at the finances, and seen their books?"

"Umm, no . . . actually, that's why I was calling you, Mark."

"What do you mean?"

"Can you come over here and look at everything for me? Check it out and see if it's as good as it looks. I'd really appreciate it. Gabriella wants me to take her to the mountains here next week and I need someone I can trust to look into this thing. Can you do it Mark?" When Ailen asked you if you can do something, there really was only one answer. He was just polite in phrasing it that way.

"Sure, Ailen. When did you want me to come over?"

"Well, honestly, I've already made you a flight reservation for tomorrow morning. Is that alright?" Mark took a deep breath but knew he couldn't refuse Ailen—and he didn't really want to, anyway. So, he said,

"Sure, that'll be fine. Send me details and let me go break the news to Niamh."

"She can come with you, Mark. The two of you can go. That's what I'd planned. I have tickets for both of you."

"No, she can't go, Ailen. Ennis is in school, and we don't want to interrupt that. I'll be fine, but thanks anyway." They worked out all the details and discussed things a little further, but Ailen never mentioned any of the businesses in Dungloe—his businesses. Before they ended the call, Mark said, "By the way, everything is great here, in case you were wondering."

Ailen answered, "I wasn't wondering. I always know everything is great there, Mark. See you soon." Mark put his phone down and then started questioning how to break the news to Niamh, and then really started worrying about how he was going to live without her in North Carolina for several days. Niamh wasn't happy with the news, but she knew Ailen, and she knew what Mark's responsibilities were with him. But she made him promise that his stay would not be more than a week, no matter what Ailen said. Heck, Mark was thinking more like three or four days. He didn't think he could make it an entire week without Niamh.

Ailen had absentmindedly made Mark's flight schedule to arrive in Charlotte, not Raleigh, where the traffic and congestion would be horrible. However, Amie and Eric had also scheduled for Sam to pick up Mark at the airport. Sam was there waiting on him and somehow navigated the quagmire and muck that the roads in Charlotte are known for. Mark didn't mean to, but he fell asleep on the drive to Winston-Salem. When Sam woke him, they were in the parking lot at Finnegan's Wake. Sam carried Mark's luggage and put it in the rental car they arranged for him, before they went inside to see Amie and Eric.

Mark immediately saw Eric behind the bar talking to a customer but didn't see Amie anywhere. Eric came around the bar and he and Mark shook hands and almost half-hugged, like men are apt to do. As they were talking, Amie came from the kitchen area and ran over to hug Mark's neck, as women are apt to do. Mark was shocked! Not that Amie was hugging him tightly, but that her hair wasn't purple any longer. It was a light brown, almost blonde color which startled Mark. When she finally pulled away, Eric said, "Come on, let's sit and get you something to drink."

They sat at a table in the corner so they could talk with each other. Mark didn't know what to say, Amie's hair color still had him rattled. He didn't want to ask her about it, he didn't exactly know how to broach a subject like that. So, he asked Eric how he was doing, Eric answered, "Well, I've been waking up grumpy for a couple of weeks now, but this morning, I let her sleep in."

Amie elbowed him on the arm and they both laughed, while Mark was still trying to figure things out. Then, Eric added, "We've got some news for you, Mark. Amie is pregnant!" With that said, they both screamed and Mark quickly stood to hug Amie again and shake Eric's hand. They immediately told him all they knew about the possible due date and what names they were discussing. Then Amie added,

"I've decided not to color my hair while I'm pregnant. I didn't want to take a chance on any hair dye having a possible effect on the baby. I didn't know if you noticed it or not."

Mark lied and said, "No, I hadn't noticed at all. Your hair looks great." Amie was beaming as Eric had a rather puzzled look on his face. Then Amie said,

"Don't worry about the pub at all, Mark. I can work until the day before delivery and then after the baby is born, I'll be back in about a week. Don't you worry, everything will be fine." Eric was nodding as Amie said all this, then he added,

"Right, don't worry, Mark. Is this okay that she's pregnant? Because, if it's not . . ."

"Whoa! Stop right there, both of you. It's not only okay, its great! I'm very happy for you and can't wait to call Niamh and tell her. However, there are two things I'm not happy with." Eric and Amie both held their breath waiting for the next sentence, as Mark continued, "Amie, you will NOT work up to the day of your delivery, you will stay home and rest. And you will NOT come back to work a week after the baby is born. Do you understand? That's not a suggestion, it's an order."

They both tried to hug Mark at the same time, it was a little awkward, but loving. Eric ordered Mark a Guinness, while he ordered Amie a Diet Sprite so they could all toast the good news together. It was a great day in Winston-Salem, North Carolina. But it could've been a whole lot better if a young lady with red-tinted hair and emerald-green eyes had been there with them to celebrate.

TbIRTY-ONE

MARK MET WITH THE OWNERS OF THE BREWERY that was for sale, Mr. and Mrs. McRacken. When Mark was shown back to their office, he said, "So nice to meet you. I'm Mark, the guy who called earlier concerning the sale of the brewery." They both smiled, stood up to shake hands, and the gentleman replied,

"Very good to meet you, Mark. I'm Mr. McRacken and this is my wife, Mrs. McRacken. Please have a seat. Would you like something to drink?" Since it was only 9:00 in the morning, Mark declined the offer, even though it seemed that Mr. and Mrs. McRacken were both sipping on something which was definitely not coffee or tea. Mark told them about Ailen and himself, then they showed him around the brewery, and offered to let him see the financials for the past year. Ailen, however, already had access to that information through his friend in Winston, Desmond Jones.

It seemed odd to Mark that the couple, who he assumed to be in their early 60's, were addressed by everyone in the brewery as Mr. and Mrs. McRacken. The couple of guys back in the distillery section, the cleaning man, a receiving person out at the dock, and one of the staff who was setting up the bar area, all referred to them as Mr. and Mrs. McRacken, never by a first name. After the tour they came back to the office and Mr. McRacken told Mark they were looking forward to doing some travelling after the sale went through. Mark asked them if they had anyplace special they wanted to see. Mr. McRacken replied, "Oh, yes, we've always wanted to go up to Grandfather Mountain and maybe even visit the Cherokee Casino up there."

Mark asked, "You've never been there before?"

"Oh, no," Mrs. McRacken replied, "We've been far too busy to take any trips like that." Mark thought to himself, *it's only three or four hours away.* Then Mr. McRacken added,

"We'd also like to visit the Outer Banks. That's on the coast here in North Carolina, in case you haven't heard of them."

"Oh, I'm familiar with the Outer Banks," Mark replied, "it's beautiful out there."

Mrs. McRacken asked, "So you've been out there, have you?"

"Yes, ma'am, I've visited several times in the past."

Then she asked him, "So you've probably been to Raleigh as well?" At this point, Mark thought they were playing with him. Raleigh was only two hours from Winston-Salem. He assumed they were conducting some sort of practical joke on him, until she continued, "Oh, we've always wanted to visit the capitol, Raleigh seems like such a nice place. We've even thought of going to Charlotte as well, but I'm getting ahead of myself now." She looked over at her husband and he grabbed her hand and they smiled at each other. Mark then knew they weren't joking at all. They were indeed very serious.

They discussed the sales details, what they were expecting, and what their lawyer had told them. Mark wrote everything down and they talked about some other details, but it was all normal and routine stuff. Mark told them he'd be back in touch as soon as he called Ailen with the details. Mr. McRacken then told him, "Take your time. We're in no hurry, and no one else has made an offer yet. Just let us know what you're thinking."

Mark thanked them for their time and hospitality and went back to his place to call Ailen. When Ailen answered, Mark told him that the sale could be completed whenever Ailen wanted to do it. Ailen told him to go back over there and do it right then. He was eager to get moving on his new venture. Mark first stopped by Finnegan's Wake to have a bite to eat and congratulate Eric and Amie again, then he walked back down the street to the brewery.

When Mark walked in the brewery, he was happy to see that customers were already starting to come in. Business was indeed good. He felt good about the sale. Mr. McRacken saw him and walked over to greet him, then said, "Didn't expect to see you back so soon, Mark. Did you forget something?"

"No, sir, not at all. I spoke with Ailen and we're both happy with everything and wanted to accept your offer and move forward with the sale." Mark expected Mr. McRacken to be very happy with this news, but instead, he replied,

"Come over here a second, Mark." He directed Mark to the back wall, away from the bar area where some customers were sitting, and said, "I'm afraid we've had another offer on the table that was considerably higher than yours. It's something we couldn't turn down, so after I called my lawyer, we accepted the offer."

Mark was shocked, he said, "But I was just here a couple of hours ago and you never mentioned anything about another offer." Mark thought that maybe Mr. McRacken was using this as a ploy to up the price of the sale.

"When we spoke earlier, I didn't have another offer. It wasn't until you left that the offer became available. Pretty sudden, if I must say."

Mark totally didn't understand what had just happened. He didn't know how to respond and was wondering how he was going to tell Ailen what was happening, when he saw his friend

Desmond sitting at the far end of the bar. Mark said, "Please give me a little while to think about this and call Ailen with the news. Can you do that, Mr. McRacken?"

"I wish I could, Mark, but I've already accepted the new offer. I really couldn't turn it down, it was more than we could have imagined. I hope you understand."

Mark said, "Just give me a few minutes to see if Ailen can match or better that offer, okay? I'll have an answer for you shortly, then you can call the other guy and give him an answer. Can you do that for me, Mr. McRacken?"

"Oh, I don't have to call him, he's sitting right over there." He was pointing at the bar area where several young, college-aged people were sitting near Desmond.

Mark looked where he was pointing and said, "They're all college kids. You're saying one of them wants to buy the brewery?"

"No, not them . . . him." Now he was pointing directly at Desmond, who had turned around on his stool and was smiling at Mark.

Mark exclaimed, "Him?"

"Yeah, he followed you in this morning and when you left, he made the offer. I couldn't believe it."

Again, Mark pointed at Desmond and asked, "Him?"

"Yes, sir, he's a great guy."

Mark left Mr. McRacken and marched over to Desmond, who was still smiling at him. Desmond stuck his hand out and said, "Mark, good to see you, dude. How are you?"

"How am I? You want to know how I am?"

"Yeah, how are you?"

"Desmond, did you just make an offer to buy this place?"

"Well, if you must know, yes, I did. What business is it of yours?"

Mark was fuming, "Do you know what Ailen's going to say when he hears about this?"

"Ahh, he'll be fine. We're good buddies. Don't worry about Ailen."

"He'll be fine?!? Are you crazy, Desmond? When Ailen hears you went behind his back, he'll chew you up and spit you out."

"I didn't go behind anyone's back. I came in here AFTER you, Mark. You had your chance to make the offer and you didn't do it. I gave you the opportunity and you blew it. I just happened to take advantage of it. That's business, Mark. Live with it."

Mark turned to leave, then stopped and looked back at Desmond, and said, "This isn't over, Desmond. When Ailen hears about this, I'd hate to be in your shoes."

ThIRTY-TWO

"Hello."

"Ailen, it's Mark, I have some bad news."

"Don't tell me that Dublin beat Galway again in the hurling championships."

"No. Worse. Your friend, Desmond, went behind our backs and bought the brewery right out from under us." There was complete silence from Ailen's end of the phone. After a minute or two, Mark asked him, "Did you hear me?" More silence, but this time Mark knew to leave it alone, and wait it out. After a few minutes, Ailen said,

"Are you sure?"

"Yes."

"I mean, are you sure it was the Desmond that I know? Could it have been someone else maybe?"

"No. I spoke with Desmond myself and he admitted it." More silence for about two minutes, then Ailen said,

"I'll call you back. Don't leave Winston-Salem yet." Mark knew this was not going to be good. For starters, Desmond was Ailen's friend. Secondly, Desmond's wife, Stella, was Ailen's wife's sister. How could it get more complicated and complex than that? Mark decided to go back to Finnegan's Wake and have a drink while he waited for Ailen's call. The pub was bustling, and Eric was busy behind the bar. Mark walked over to a small table near the coatrack and sat down. Before he barely got settled, Amie had come over and sat down with him. She was smiling broadly and asked him how he was. He didn't want to bring up the brewery thing yet, so he said, "I'm fine, Amie. How are you today?"

She was absentmindedly rubbing her stomach, which showed no signs of pregnancy yet, when she answered, "We want eight."

"You want eight what?" Mark had no idea what she was referring to.

She smiled brightly and continued, "We want eight children!"

Mark was understandably taken aback, and asked, "You want eight children?"

"Yes! Eight!!"

"That sounds marvelous, Amie, but maybe you should wait until you have the first one and then decide on how many more you want."

"Nope, we're gonna have eight, Mark. It's settled." At this point, Mark looked over to the bar where Eric was working, however, he wasn't really working—he was looking at Amie and Mark. Mark stared at him and raised his eyebrows, Eric half-shrugged his shoulders until he saw Amie also look over at him, then he beamed brightly and yelled out,

"Eight!" Mark didn't know what else to say, so he smiled while Amie continued rubbing her stomach. Then she said,

"Now don't you worry, Mark. We have it all figured out . . . we're going to turn the side office into a nursery. That way I can always be here helping out and check on the babies. And Eric will be here fulltime. It'll be perfect! I don't want you to worry about anything, Mark. We've got it all figured out. No problem."

Mark kept smiling and nodding, but he wanted to ask: *How are you going to raise eight kids? And that's at least nine, or ten, or twelve years it'll take to do that. And eight kids? Are you crazy, girl?* But he kept quiet. He knew that she was still in the enthusiastic, elation-filled frenzy of her first pregnancy. Once she went through the drama and sickness of pregnancy, then the pain of delivery, certainly she would change her mind. Wouldn't she?

Before anything else was said, Mark's phone rang, it was Ailen. Mark said, "Excuse me, I have to take this." He walked outside to have some quiet and privacy, and answered, "Hey, got anything figured out yet?"

Ailen sounded excited as he said, "Yes! Let Desmond have the brewery." Mark figured Ailen's wife, the beautiful Gabriella, had convinced him not to do anything to harm her sister's husband. Then Ailen continued, "We'll build our own brewery! We'll build one on the next corner and compete with him. If he charges five dollars for a beer, we'll charge four dollars. If he opens at twelve, we'll open at eleven. If he has a food truck stationed there, we'll have two food trucks. We'll make him wish he'd never woke up this morning." Mark was stunned. He never expected this. He also knew that to accomplish all Ailen wanted, he would be spending a lot more time in Winston-Salem in the near future.

* * *

The first thing Mark did was call Niamh and explain everything to her. She wasn't mad at the news, but she wasn't happy either. She filled him in on everything happening in Dungloe, including Ennis, her parents, the businesses, and the local gossip. Then she told Mark to finish what he had to do today and call her back tonight—not too late though, because of the five-hour time difference. He next called the pub to check on Siobhan and make sure she was okay. She was. In fact, she told Mark that they had more sales in the last two weeks than the pub had in the previous month. Then he called the restaurant to speak with Claire, only she wasn't there, which was very unusual. He told the young guy who answered the phone to get a message to her and tell her to return his call.

He sat there for half-a-minute thinking about what he needed to do next when his phone rang—Claire. He answered and she said, "What do you want, Mark? Do you not trust me?"

"Yes, I trust you, Claire. I just wanted to touch base and see how things were. Is everything okay?"

"Of course, everything is okay, I'm not some brand, new employee who wears inappropriate clothing, walking around making a mockery of herself, embarrassing the business, and staining the culture of our hometown, now am I?"

He knew that however he answered that question would cause a turmoil, so instead of answering, he asked another question, "Claire, look, I really need an experienced person, someone accomplished and effective in business affairs, and being strong and influential in the community, to do me a huge favor. Do you think you can help?"

"Well, of course I can, Mark. What do you need?"

He had her now, which was great, except that he didn't know what to say next. Before he stumbled too much, he quickly said, "Hold on, Claire, Ailen's trying to call me, I'm going to have to take his call. Please keep your phone handy and I'll call you back as soon as Ailen and I agree on our next move. Okay?"

"Sure, Mark, tell Ailen that you can count on me. Anything at all, just let me know."

"Great, Claire, I'll call you back soon." He quickly disconnected the call hoping he could think of something to satisfy her ego and expectations before he called her back.

* * *

Desmond did buy the brewery, but it took all he had to make the deal. He and Stella were in up to their ears with debt now. Mark spent the next couple of weeks meeting with the owners of two old tobacco warehouses near Fiddlin' Fish. Both were within two blocks of the Fish and each had the space and necessities to be converted into breweries, with enough money, which Ailen had.

Mark met with both ownership groups several times and made offers for both buildings—offers below the asking prices that were listed. One group wouldn't budge. The other group, which was headed by the grandson of an executive from the old days of RJ Reynolds Tobacco, did negotiate. Ailen ended up getting the property for about 18% below asking price. The family was tired of paying taxes on the old building year after year, and just wanted to get rid of it.

Finally, Mark could go home and see his family. Niamh drove to Shannon to meet Mark at the airport, where they had a long embrace, with tears from each of them. Mark drove them back to Dungloe. No stopping at the Cliffs of Moher to see the beautiful ocean views. No stopping at the ancient castles on the way through the countryside. No stopping at the many lakes and streams to stare at the green tinted countryside. No stopping at the many roadside pubs they passed on the way. And no stopping to say hello, or check-in, with Siobhan or Claire . . . no. Mark drove straight home, to their home, to their castle, to their life, to their bedroom, to their dreams.

THIRTY-THREE

EACH WEEK MARK WOULD GET UPDATES from the company they hired to convert the old warehouse into a brewery. And updates, as well as pictures, from Amie on her expanding waistline as the pregnancy progressed. Both Amie's due date and the completion of the brewery were expected in the same month. Mark didn't have to return to Winston-Salem until everything was finalized. Eric had the financial background to handle things in between. Siobhan had the pub running so well that Mark thought about expanding the seating area to accommodate their ever-growing customer base. And, strangely enough, Claire was unexpectedly calm and fairly easy to communicate with. Everything seemed smooth and easy in Mark's life. Until . . .

He had trained the bartender to always have coffee brewing each morning when he arrived, so all he had to do was come in, sit down, pour his coffee, and add a little milk. Just as he took his first sip, this morning, his cell phone rang. It was Niamh, whom he just left less than an hour ago, she said, "Mark, are you sitting down?" Which he thought was a rather odd question, but he answered,

"Yes, why?"

"I'm pregnant! We're going to have a baby! You're going to be a father!" The next thing Mark remembers is someone waking him up as he was lying on the couch back in the office of the pub. There was a wet towel on his forehead and Siobhan was holding his hand, while checking his pulse. He heard her say,

"He's waking up. Call Niamh back and tell her he's okay." Mark sat up and was looking at the coffee stains on his shirt and pants when Niamh came in the door. She had rushed over when Siobhan first called her. She sat beside him and took both his hands and asked him if he was okay.

"Yeah, I'm fine. What happened?

Siobhan said, "You were drinking your coffee and then you just fell on the floor. Are you sure you're alright?"

Mark answered, "Yeah, I feel fine . . . why did I fall on the . . ." Then, he remembered why he fell on the floor. He suddenly looked over at Niamh, then down at her stomach, then back at her face, and asked, "Is it true?" Niamh couldn't answer because she started crying. They hugged each other as Siobhan, the cook, and two waitresses were standing there wondering what was happening. Then Mark jumped up from the couch and yelled "We're pregnant!" Niamh rose and everyone started hugging everyone around her. Then, the rest of the staff and a few customers came in to see what was happening, and soon everyone in the entire pub was hugging everyone else.

Someone obviously called Claire, because within a few minutes she came in the door holding a Banoffee pie in each hand, which happened to be Mark's favorite dessert in the world. Mark's face was set in a permanent smile. He was so happy he couldn't even taste the Banoffee. He kept telling everyone who came in, "We're pregnant! We're going to have a baby." Even Claire hugged his neck and said,

"I'm proud of you, Mark. I didn't know you had it in you." And, for once, she wasn't being mean or curt, she was only saying what was truly in her mind. Claire was even thoughtful, as she saved a piece of Banoffee for Mark, for when the festivities died down a little. Everyone celebrated with a Guinness or a shot of Irish whiskey—everyone except Niamh, who only had a cup of tea. Then, as people started to filter out, Mark decided to call Ailen and tell him the news.

Mark dialed Ailen's number, but his wife, Gabriella, answered the call. Mark was bursting with excitement and couldn't wait to tell his best friend about his good news. When she answered, Mark said, "Gabriella, can I speak to Ailen please, I have some great news."

Four or five seconds of silence, then she said, "No, you can't speak to him, Mark."

"C'mon, Gabs, he's going to love this—trust me!"

"Mark . . . Ailen is dead."

"C'mon, quit joking. Let me speak to him." Silence from her end, then Mark heard a quiet sobbing. He said, rather loudly,

"Gabriella? Are you there? What's happening? Gabriella?" Niamh sensed something was wrong and came over to put her arm around Mark's arm. Again, Mark said, "Gabriella?"

"Yes, I'm here, Mark. I'm sorry to have to tell you this, but Ailen is dead. He never woke up this morning. We had a great dinner last night, and a couple of drinks, then watched a movie on television before we went to bed. Everything seemed so perfect . . . but it wasn't." Mark asked,

"What happened?"

"We went to bed and fell asleep rather quickly, as we always do, but Ailen never woke up. I usually get up a little earlier than he does, so I did, and went in to make us some tea. When I went back to the bedroom to bring it to him, I noticed something wrong. He wasn't moving. He wasn't doing anything. I knew it then. He was dead. I checked his pulse—nothing. I pounded on his chest and tried mouth-to-mouth, but nothing helped. It was too late. I called for an ambulance, but he was already cold, Mark. He was already cold." She started crying again as Mark held the phone to his ear in a stunned silence.

Somehow, without Mark saying a word to her, Niamh knew as well. She put both her arms around Mark and started a slow sob of her own. Mark never heard anything else from Gabriella for at least three or four minutes, so he disconnected the call. He'd call back later. Everyone in the room knew something was wrong—terribly wrong. When Mark told them all the news, everyone in the pub was crying—even Claire. Ailen was not only their boss and owner of the businesses, but he was also their friend for many years. Finally, Siobhan asked, "What happened, Mark?"

"Apparently, they went to bed last night, but Ailen never woke up. He died during the night. He was dead when Gabriella woke this morning." All the women in the pub started crying and all the men wanted to. Ailen was their friend, mentor, and someone they all admired.

The pub went from outrageous joy over Mark and Niamh's news, to uncontrollable sorrow from Ailen's death. Mark finally put his phone down and hugged Niamh in silence, while she was crying a little harder. Mark didn't know if he would start crying or start screaming. He thought to himself how thankful he should be for what he had, because in one moment, like now, your entire life could change.

* * *

Ailen's funeral closed the entire town for three days. The pub, the restaurants, and every other business was closed, and everyone in town was in mourning. The funeral itself filled the huge Catholic church in town, plus all the streets surrounding the church, as well as the small Baptist church, where the pastor, GC, held a special service for Ailen. It would take a long time, if ever, for Dungloe to recover from this tragedy. Ailen not only owned the most profitable businesses in town, but all the others depended on him for financing and support.

It took several weeks for people to even start smiling again. Claire and Siobhan both wore nothing but black for at least two weeks, albeit Siobhan's skirts and dresses were much shorter and extremely less Amish-looking than Claire's. Even Jims, in the neighboring town, closed his pub for several days, not because he and Ailen were such good friends, but rather because of his long and deep friendship with Mark. Into the third week after the funeral, Gabriella called and asked Mark to come out to her house by the bay, so they could discuss the businesses and how they'd go forward.

Mark had no idea what to expect from this meeting. He owned nothing. He simply managed the businesses for Ailen. He assumed Gabriella now owned everything and how things would go forward was completely up to her. He had no idea what she was thinking or what she wanted. When he arrived, Gabriella was still dressed in black pants with a black blouse. However, she did seem a little more normal and less somber than she had in the last two weeks. She led him out to the bay window, which overlooked the inlet where several small islands dotted the coastline.

She had a pot of tea for her and pot of coffee for Mark sitting on the table between the two chairs. After the initial welcoming and asking how each was coping, she got right down to business, "Mark, as you probably guessed, since Ailen had no other family, he left almost everything to me. Almost everything. He had much more than I realized. I always knew of the businesses and investments he had, but not exactly how much they were all worth. Ailen was a wealthy man. Let me rephrase that, he was an extremely wealthy man."

Mark already knew most of this, not the exact numbers, but he knew Ailen had done very well and invested even better. Gabriella continued, "As you know, I grew up in Winston-

Salem. I love it here in Ireland, but North Carolina is my home, and that's where I'm going to live." This didn't surprise Mark at all. "Mark, I trust you, just as Ailen did, and I want you to continue doing just as you've been doing, with one change." Mark suddenly tensed, wondering what she had in mind. She refilled her teacup, then took a small sip, and set it back down, then looked at Mark and continued, "I want us to be in business together. I'm going to have my lawyer draw up papers making you one-third owner of all the businesses in Ireland and Winston-Salem." It'll be more money than you're being paid now—much more."

Mark was startled and said, "Gabriella, maybe you should take some time and think about all this before you make any type of permanent decision."

She looked at him and said, "Can I continue to always trust you, Mark, just as Ailen trusted you?"

"Of course, you can, you know that."

"Then it's settled. This way I won't have to worry about any business partners trying to cheat me, and I won't have to spend all my time running the businesses, which were never my interests anyway. It's what you do. It's what you've always done. Why change things? I just don't want to be bothered with the everyday headaches of it all, Mark. It's what you do, not me. I trust you. Will you do it?"

Mark's head was spinning. It was a lot more responsibility, plus, it was now HIS responsibility, and HIS money, and HIS future. He stood up and said, "I'd love to. Thank you for trusting me, Gabriella. I will never let you down, I hope you know that."

Gabriella stood and hugged Mark's neck, then stood back and put her hand forward to shake Mark's hand, and said, "Thanks, partner."

THIRTY-FOUR

GABRIELLA WENT BACK TO WINSTON-SALEM after all the details of her merger with Mark were finalized. For her, it was a great deal: she didn't have to worry with the day-to-day operations of all the businesses, which she wasn't interested in or familiar with. Plus, she trusted Mark and knew he would always do the right thing. She would now involve herself in the arts district of Winston, which had been her passion ever since she graduated from the North Carolina School of the Arts, with a degree in ballet and dance.

When the attorney explained everything to Mark, he was overwhelmed. He was now worth more than he ever dreamed of. Niamh, too, was staggered at how much Mark now had. She kept asking him, "Is this real? Are you sure it's all yours?"

"No, honey, it's not all mine . . . it's OURS!" It was hard for them to fathom what had just happened. Mark tried his best to explain to Niamh how it all worked out: "I didn't get any cash from Ailen and Gabriella, so we can't go out and buy a new house or anything. What I got was one-third ownership of all the businesses. So, if everything stays profitable, here and in North Carolina, we should start seeing some pretty good returns coming in. I guess it's all a matter of how well the businesses do." In essence, Mark and Niamh's financial future was in the hands of Siobhan, Claire, Amie and Eric, and the few others who managed the businesses. Mark felt good.

After the funeral was over and everything started to operate normally again, he stopped by the Feed and Grain store to check in and say hello. When he walked in the door, the manager, Guarino, said, "Mark, I've got a question to ask you."

"Sure, Guarino, go ahead."

"Am I going to get a raise?"

Mark frowned and asked, "Why are you asking me that? You know we give yearly raises out the first week of December. It's what we've always done, Guarino."

"Well, I thought that now since you were totally in charge of things, we might reevaluate how things work now."

Mark nodded and stepped closer to Guarino, then answered, "That's a great idea, Guarino, let me go back to the office and see just how profitable the business has been this year. I'll take a close look at that and then we can adjust your pay either up or down, depending on how business has been. How's that sound?"

Guarino knew the feed and grain business was not growing at all. In fact, he often wondered why Ailen kept it open as long as he has. He quickly said, "Naw, that's okay Mark. I was just wondering, it's not important. We'll just keep things as they are. I don't want you to do any extra work checking on things just for me. By the way, I hear you're going to be a father soon. Congratulations!"

Exactly the response Mark was hoping for. Guarino then went to the cooler and got Mark a Diet Pepsi, "On the house!" just to show Mark how much he liked him. Wasn't that nice? Mark took his Diet Pepsi and left the store as he walked down the street toward the pub. Since the rain had stopped, he decided to sit on one of the benches along the main street and sip his Diet Pepsi. It wasn't long before one of the young girls who worked at the pub passed him on her way to work. She said hello and then asked, "Sir, do you think we'll be getting any sort of bonus, or maybe even a raise since you're taking over?"

Mark stood up and answered, "Kali, tell me, why do think you should be getting a bonus right now? Or a raise?"

"Well, sir, I just thought that, you know, since you're now, umm, you know . . . "

"No, I don't know at all."

She fumbled with her purse, then brushed her hair back a little, before saying, "Well, it's been nice seeing you, sir. Take care, I've got to be going—don't want to be late." She quickly turned and hustled down the street as Mark thought to himself, *if they're acting like this, what in the world is Claire going to be up to?*

He walked past the pub, which he hadn't planned on, just so he could go to the restaurant and confront Claire and set things straight with her as well. He knew this could get very ugly, very quickly, and he wanted to get it over with. When he walked in, the restaurant still had a nice crowd seated, at least three quarters full, but one of the waitresses said, "Over here, sir, I have a table ready for you." This was odd, since Claire always asked him if he had a reservation before she would seat him.

As he sat down, another waitress brought him a hot cup of coffee and a large piece of Banoffee pie. He still didn't see Claire anywhere, but the waitress said, "Miss Claire said she'd be right out, sir. You go ahead and enjoy your meal. If you need anything else, just look for me and I'll be right over."

Okay, Mark thought, *what's going on here?* He sipped his coffee and tasted the Banoffee, which was wonderful, as usual, then he saw Claire coming over toward him. He started to stand up, but she said, "Stay seated, sir, enjoy your dessert. Do you mind if I sit with you?"

"Please . . . I was just passing by and thought I'd stop and see if you needed anything. Is everything good?"

Claire smiled brightly and replied, "Yes, we're doing great. Don't you worry about a thing, Mark. Anytime you need anything from me, just let me know. Now if you don't need me, I really need to get back to the kitchen, if you don't mind."

"No, Claire, no problem. Good to see you." She smiled brightly again, then walked back to the kitchen area as Mark sat there thinking, *what in the world is happening here?*

He finally made it to the pub, where the bartender had a cup of coffee ready for him. He really didn't want another cup but took it just to be polite. Everyone in the pub acted normally, even Siobhan, who came over to have him sign some invoices. However, Mark did notice that whenever he looked around, everyone in the pub was staring at him. As soon as he would catch their gaze, they'd turn away. After the second time of catching Siobhan quickly turn away from him, he called over to her, "Hey, Siobhan, come over here." She smiled and walked over, and Mark said, "Here, sit down a minute."

When she sat, she crossed her legs rather slowly and easily viewable for Mark to see—if he chose to. She said, "Yes, Mark, what's up?"

"Okay, Siobhan, what's going on with everyone?"

"I don't know what you're talking about."

"Yes, you do. Tell me now or I'll sit here with you all day until you talk."

The smile faded from her face. After a slight pause, she said, "Look, Mark, things are different now that you're the owner. It was different when you were just the manager of things, but now you OWN things. It's different!" Mark didn't know how to respond. They both sat there looking down at the table, each of them wondering what to say, and more importantly, what to do. After several awkward moments, Siobhan got up and walked back to the bar. Mark continued to sit and wonder. This was going to be harder than he thought it would.

* * *

Back in Winston-Salem, Eric and Amie were experiencing a little difficulty, not with Finnegan's, but with their first-time pregnancy. Amie had somehow taken the effects of "morning sickness" to a new level. She threw up in the morning, she threw up after lunch, and she really threw up after dinner. Eric was distraught because there was nothing he could do to help or make the sickness stop. They tried the doctor, which was not much help at all. He prescribed her some pills to take and advised her to stop working so much. As soon as she would take one of the pills, she would throw it up within an hour. And Eric did everything he could to try and keep her at home and out of the pub—nothing worked.

One afternoon, after she had thrown up in the women's bathroom at Finnegan's, Eric tried to comfort her and said, "This certainly is a lot harder than we thought it would be. I'm not sure either of us can do this eight times."

"Yes, we are, Eric! Do you hear me? Eight! We're going to have eight kids if I have to puke out every organ in my body! Do you understand me?"

"Sure, Honey, just calm down. We'll do eight . . . just calm down and take it easy."

"Eight, Eric! And I mean it."

"Got it. Now, I've been thinking about a name for the baby, what do you think about Shelley if it's a girl, or Mark if it's a boy? We could name it after Mark who has helped us out so much. What do you think?"

Amie took a slow drink of something from a thermos bottle, then said, "We're naming this baby, Jacob."

"Jacob?"

"Yes, Jacob."

"Okay . . . but what if it's a girl?"

Amy set her bottle down and said, "It's not going to be a girl. It's going to be a boy and its name is going to be Jacob. Do you understand?" Eric nodded, now knowing that this baby would definitely be a boy, if it knows what's good for itself, or else. And . . . Jacob was alright with him, that was a good name. As soon as that was settled, Amie left quickly for the bathroom once more, as Eric thought to himself, *seven more times after this? Oh, my God!*

THIRTY-FIVE

SIX MONTHS AFTER THE FUNERAL, Gabriella was still having a difficult time adjusting to life without Ailen. Just as she was his life, he was also her life. She had many interests, which included the School of the Arts, her sister, and many activities that she and Ailen were involved in, but that was the issue: activities that she and AILEN were involved in. She was lost without him . . . well, not lost, but directionless and without momentum. It was a tough transition for her. Initially, she would call Mark once a week, simply to get an update on the businesses, never to offer advice. However, lately, it was more like once a month, and then it was mostly to check on him and Niamh and her pregnancy, seldom about any business issues.

Mark missed Ailen as well. Ever since his arrival in Ireland, Ailen was the one person Mark could always count on for help, for inspiration, for friendship, and for support. Fortunately, he now had Niamh, whereas Gabriella only had her memories and her broken heart. Several times, Mark caught himself absentmindedly picking up the phone to call Ailen to discuss something about the business, only to be reminded of his own loss.

Eric and Amie had Finnegan's running well and work was being completed on the new brewery down the street from Fiddlin' Fish. Amie's sickness due to the pregnancy never subsided, she continued to throw up daily, though now it was only once or twice, not three or four times each day. The delivery date for Jacob was only four or five weeks away now. Amie had refused to let the doctor's give her the exam to determine if the baby was a boy or girl—no need—she KNEW it was a boy . . . she was sure of it. Eric hoped it was a boy, he prayed every night, *Lord, please let this baby be healthy, and please—pretty please-- let it be a boy.*

Mark was planning on going back to Winston-Salem for the arrival of the baby, which happened to coincide with the completion of the new brewery, which would be named, "Ailen's." He wouldn't be able to stay long in Winston because his own child was due to be born soon after Amie's baby. Niamh was having a healthy pregnancy and she, like Amie, didn't want to have the test done to see if it was a boy or girl. She wanted them to be surprised.

Everything else in Dungloe was routine, happy, and predictable. Siobhan, and her short skirts, were the major attraction at the pub, which had to add a side room to accommodate all the men in town. Claire had the restaurant running as usual: efficient, profitable, and popular. There was some discussion in town that she had even taken to wearing some makeup at times, though no one could be entirely sure of that, and certainly, no one would ever ask her that question.

Guarino kept his feed store open, though Mark thought several times about closing it. It barely broke even most months, and certainly there was not much of a future for it. But Guarino was loyal, so Mark would let it go for a while and hope things turned around. His friend over in Burtonport, Jims, was thinking of retiring and asked Mark if he wanted to buy his pub from him. Mark was very interested, but certainly didn't have the cash to make that deal. He told Jims he would discuss it with Gabriella and let him know. Jims was in no hurry to sell to a stranger, but he would love for Mark to have it.

* * *

So, that's how things stood as Mark made his plans to travel to North Carolina several weeks later for the birth of Amie's son (hopefully), and the opening of the brewery. He was excited and nervous, only because Niamh was due to deliver their child in the next few weeks as well. As usual, when Mark landed in Raleigh, Sam was there to pick him up. On the ride to Winston-Salem, they talked about Amie's baby and Sam asked Mark, "How can she be so sure it's going to be a boy? I mean, she's told everyone that her baby is going to be a boy, Mark. How can she know that? She hasn't had any tests to prove anything. I don't understand."

"Sam, there's one thing you need to learn early: we, as men, can never and will never, understand women. It's impossible. Trust me, if Amie says that baby is going to be a boy, then it's going to be a boy. That poor baby has no chance of being a girl." Sam nodded and never took his eyes off the road. He never acknowledged that he believed Mark, or not. He just kept on driving.

When they arrived in town, Sam first drove them over to the new brewery so Mark could see how it looked. Then they went to Finnegan's, which was very full, a sign that Wake Forest students were back in school. Eric met them at the door with a firm handshake, then a mighty hug for Mark. He said, "Amie's in the bathroom, she just threw up again. I'll be glad when this baby is born."

Mark said, "I hope she's okay. How do you think she'll be if the baby turns out to be a girl?"

Eric froze, then added, "It better not be. She's already started buying boy's clothes, Mark. This baby HAS to be a boy . . . it HAS to."

Mark nodded and patted Eric on the shoulder, telling him, "I'm sure she knows. Women have a way of knowing things like that. They can tell. Don't worry, it'll be a boy."

Eric asked, "Really?"

Mark nodded and said, "What do you think? That baby would NEVER consider disobeying Amie, would it?"

Before Eric could consider an answer, Amie came from the back, where the bathroom was, and rushed forward to hug Mark's neck. He was astonished at how big she was. Her stomach was much larger than Niamh's was, but she looked great and happy, especially for a woman who had spent the last nine months throwing up every day. They all went back to the office and caught up with each other's news, then discussed the business, and the brewery. Eric had done an outstanding job with the finances of each, and the brewery was scheduled for the Grand Opening this coming Saturday.

After dinner, Mark went to the Cardinal hotel and called Niamh, checking on her. Then he called Gabriella to check in with her as well. Both were doing fine, so he decided to go down to the hotel bar and have a drink, then go to bed early. The day's events had worn him out. Gabriella had invited him to stay at her house, but he didn't feel comfortable with that. He'd rather stay at the hotel and rest. When he checked in, he went downstairs to the bar, where hotel guests had access to the free wine tasting. He had just ordered a glass of Muscadine wine when his phone rang. It was Eric.

"Mark, it's happening. Her water broke and we're going to the hospital. See you there." He disconnected the call before Mark could say anything or ask him which hospital they were going to. Mark set his wine down and rushed outside where a couple of taxis were waiting. The driver asked where and Mark said,

"Baptist Hospital." The driver knew a route that skipped most of the stoplights, and within a few minutes, they arrived at the drop off zone, where he asked,

"Do you want me to wait for you?"

"No, I'll be a while, thanks for asking." Mark paid him and rushed into the receptionist desk area and asked for Amie's room number. She said,

"Don't have anyone here by that name."

"She's having a baby, maybe she doesn't have a room number yet."

The receptionist called down to the emergency room section and was told no one had come in having a baby in the last six hours. Then she said, "Are you sure she's at this hospital?"

"No, I'm not." He thanked her and rushed back outside to see if the taxi was still there. It wasn't. He was told that the next taxi would probably arrive in the next 10-15 minutes. Fifteen minutes can seem like a lifetime when you're in a hurry. Finally, a cab came up and Mark hopped in and told the driver to take him to Forsyth Hospital, which was about a twenty-minute ride from Baptist Hospital. The problem was that this driver didn't take any backroads, he went down the parkway and caught every stoplight that had ever been installed. Mark was nearly ready to jump out and start running.

Finally, they arrived, Mark paid the driver, jumped out, and ran into the hospital. He was told Amie was in the delivery section of the emergency room. He ran down the halls and asked directions and was guided to a room off the main section, where he saw Eric standing in the doorway. He walked up and tapped Eric on the shoulder. Eric never moved. Mark tapped him a little harder and Eric turned around and hugged Mark, saying, "I'm a daddy, Mark! I'm a daddy. Can you believe it?"

Mark looked around him to see a nurse standing over Amie, who was lying in the bed holding a tiny little bundle, all wrapped up and with a head covering. She never took her eyes off the baby and didn't see Mark. Eric said, "Honey, Mark's here." She still never took her eyes off the baby. Mark asked,

"Is everybody healthy?"

"Yeah, we're all fine."

Mark was almost afraid to ask the next question, but as he was looking at Eric, Eric volunteered the answer he knew Mark was interested in, "Mark, meet Jacob, my son."

TᴅIRTY-SIX

AMIE FINALLY LET ERIC HOLD HIS SON, for a minute or two; then she let Mark hold little Jacob for half a minute. He had beautiful blue eyes like his mother, and dark hair like his father, although it could have been the same color as Amie's hair, except no one really knew what color Amie's hair truly was. The nurse came in and said it was time for breastfeeding instructions, so Mark left the family in a happy glow. He had just stepped inside the elevator when his phone rang. The door closed just as he realized the call was from Niamh.

It took a minute or two for him to reach ground level and by then she had disconnected the call. He tried calling her back, but she didn't answer, which was strange, even more strange was the fact that he had a call waiting from Claire. He tried calling Niamh again, still no answer, so he called Claire to see what type of drama she was inventing now. She answered not with "Hello," but "Where are you?"

"I'm at the hospital with some friends, why?"

"Because Niamh has been trying to call you. Why wouldn't you answer?"

"Why was Niamh trying to call me? I just spoke to her this afternoon."

Claire almost started screaming, "Because she went into labor and they're taking her to the hospital!"

Mark didn't comprehend that statement . . . it sounded as though Claire said, "she went into labor . . ." But that couldn't be right, she's not due for another month. Claire continued, "Did you hear me, Mark? She's gone into labor."

"That can't be right, Claire. She's not due yet. Are you sure you have your facts right?"

"She called me when you wouldn't answer. That's what she told me, Mark." Silence on the other end, "Mark? Mark, are you there?" Oh, he was there alright, the phone was in his hand as he was running through the hospital and out the door looking for a cab. He jumped in the taxi and said,

"Take me to the airport, NOW!"

The taxi driver looked in the rearview mirror and asked, "The Winston airport?"

"No, Raleigh, the Raleigh airport."

The driver answered, "I ain't going to Raleigh mister. They'll fire me for that."

"I'll pay you, whatever you say, just take me to Raleigh."

"I told you, I ain't going to Raleigh. Now you just better get out before I call the police."

Mark got out of the cab and then remembered he had Sam's number in his call list. He quickly called him and asked, "Sam, this is Mark, what are you doing?"

"I'm sort of on a date. What's wrong?" He could tell by Mark's voice and urgency that something was going on.

Mark said, "Can you take me to Raleigh?"

"Mmm, like when?"

"Like right now! It's an emergency, Sam. I really need you."

Sam stalled a moment, then asked, "Can Rhylan come with us?"

"Can WHAT come with us?"

Sam repeated, "Rhylan, she's my girlfriend."

"You have a girlfriend named Rhylan?" Before Sam could answer, Mark said, "Yes! Bring her. I need to go right now."

Sam asked, "What time does your flight leave?"

Mark suddenly thought, *Flight?*

Sam put his phone on speakerphone and asked again, "What time is your flight, Mark?" There was no flight time because Mark hadn't made a reservation.

"Just take me there, Sam, I'll buy a ticket when I get there."

"Mark, are you sure there are flights leaving for Ireland tonight? If so, are there any vacancies?" Mark didn't know how to answer, or what to do. All he knew was that Niamh was going to the hospital to give birth to their child and he WASN'T there! As his mind was spinning, Rhylan said,

"I just checked online, there aren't any flights to either Dublin or Shannon tonight, but there is a flight to Paris, if you want it."

"I don't want to go to Paris, Rhiannon, I want to go to Ireland."

"My name is Rhylan, not Rhiannon, and I know that, sir. You can fly to Paris, then get a connecting flight to Dublin and be there in the morning. Do you want me to book it?"

"Yes! Book it now, book it right now."

"Okay, I'll need your credit card number."

Mark fumbled around his wallet, then got his card and repeated the number for her saying, "Thanks, Ryan, I really appreciate it. Book the first open flight they have."

Rhylan started to correct him again, but she knew he was flustered. Sam drove above the speed limit, but not too much above, so as not to get a ticket. Mark arrived at the gate without a coat, without any suitcases, and without anything except a mind full of worry. He had about a two hour wait for the flight to Paris and tried calling Niamh's number several times with no answer. Then he had the afterthought to call Niamh's mother. No answer there either. Before the plane started loading, he tried calling Claire again. No answer from her either. Mark was pacing around the terminal, about to go crazy, only the actual boarding of the plane saved him.

He sat in the middle seat of the five-seat section. Two strangers on his left and two strangers on his right. Each of them wondering why this man had no carryon luggage. Everybody had carryon luggage, even little kids. One of the passengers got up from his seat, he said, to go to the restroom before the flight pulled away from the gate, but he didn't really go to the bathroom, he went to see the head flight attendant. The man said, "Look, I don't want to cause any problems, but I don't want to get blown up over the Atlantic Ocean either."

The flight attendant, who was a lady in her mid-50's with about twenty-five years of experience said, "We don't joke about things like that, sir. What exactly are you talking about?"

"The man in our row, sitting in the middle, by himself, doesn't have any luggage—no carryon stuff at all. Not even a coat."

This got her attention, she asked, "Are you sure? Maybe he put something in the overhead compartment that you didn't notice."

"No ma'am. He was in front of me in the line and he never had anything. Plus, he was nervous as all get out. He's up to something and y'all need to check him out."

She told the man to go back to his seat, that she would investigate further. She then went to the cockpit and told the flight crew about the man's suspicions. The copilot called the terminal and asked about the man sitting in that seat, Mark. The woman at the desk said, "Yes, he bought the ticket online, rushed into the terminal without any luggage whatsoever, then he's been pacing and acting nervously the entire time he's been here. We all noticed him."

The copilot said, "Call airport security right now, get them down here. We won't leave the gate until they arrive. This guy needs to be checked out."

A few minutes later, Mark noticed two uniformed guards entering the plane and walking down the aisles, one of them on each side of his section. He could have sworn they were both looking directly at him. They were. When they arrived at his row, one of them told the two passengers to get up and move away, then the guard looked at Mark and said, "Come with me, sir."

Mark asked, "Me?"

"Yes, sir, you. Please come with me right now."

"Why?"

"Sir, you can get up from your seat right now, peacefully, or we'll take you out forcefully. Do you understand?"

Mark again asked, "Why? What's going on?"

That was it, both guards jumped on Mark, one of them handcuffed his arms behind him, and the other man put him in a choke hold. All the passengers were either screaming or videoing the entire ugly mess. They dragged Mark off the plane and put him in a golf cart, then drove him away. The entire time, Mark kept asking them why and what was going on. They didn't answer. At the end of terminal, they escorted Mark into a large room where four other men in suits were waiting. They took

Mark's wallet and checked his pockets. One of the men said, "He's clean."

Mark screamed, "Clean? Clean of what? What's going on here?"

"Just calm down, sir, we only want to ask you a few questions."

For the next hour they interrogated Mark and checked his identity and history. They were intrigued that he was now an Irish citizen, as well as an American citizen. Finally, after several phone calls to Ireland and Winston-Salem, they determined Mark was telling the truth and not a danger. The problem was that the flight to Paris was gone and there wasn't another until tomorrow.

ThIRTY-SEVEN

MARK FLEW TO PARIS THE NEXT MORNING, then found the next connecting flight to Dublin, and booked it. He wanted to fly to Shannon, which was closer to Dungloe, but there wasn't a flight until later in the afternoon. He called the rental car place in Dublin and booked a car upon his arrival, so he could drive himself as fast as he possibly could to the hospital, where his wife was giving birth to their child. The flight itself was not long, but it seemed interminable to Mark. He kept looking out the window to see if he could spot the coastline of Ireland as they approached, but it was too cloudy to see anything. Finally, the flaps on the wings started to extend and lower, then the wheels came down, and they landed safely at the airport in Dublin.

Mark ran off the plane and down the terminal until he spotted the rental car agency he had called. He had to wait in line behind an Englishman who was arguing with the agent about the cost of his car. Mark had a few unpleasant thoughts about the English, but wisely kept his thoughts to himself. Finally, he made it to the agent and said, "Thank goodness I'm here. I made a reservation for a mid-sized car, Mark McCarty."

"Oh, yes, Mr. McCarty, we have your reservation right here." Then the agent shuffled some papers around and said, "Unfortunately, we don't have any cars available right now."

It took Mark several seconds to comprehend what he just heard, then he said, "But I have a reservation. You just told me you had my reservation."

"Yes, sir, I do have your reservation, we just don't have any cars right now. One should be available before too long though."

"Describe *too long*."

"Oh, I'd say we should have a car ready for you in less than eight hours."

Mark almost choked as he exclaimed, "Eight hours?"

"Yes, sir, we should have one by then."

Mark put his arms up on the counter and said, in a loud voice, "But I have a reservation. That means you're supposed to hold a car for me."

The agent leaned back in his chair and replied, "I know what a reservation is, sir."

"I don't think you do! If you did, then I'd have a car waiting for me!"

The agent was getting a little flustered and said, "Let me go see the manager. Hold on." He walked back to an office, went in, and shut the door. About three minutes later, a middle-aged woman came out with the agent, walked up to Mark, and said,

"I'm sorry, sir, but there has been an influx of reservations since yesterday. We apologize and assure you that we will have a car available in about seven or eight hours."

Mark lowered his voice and leaned in close to the woman and said, "But I made a reservation. That means you're supposed to hold me a car. Do you understand that, ma'am?"

"Yes, sir, I totally understand what a reservation means. But we've had more reservations than we have cars available. Do YOU understand that?"

The North Carolina redneck in Mark truly wanted to jump out and curse like a hillbilly drinking moonshine, but it didn't. Mark said, "Oh, I understand that you don't have any cars available. And I also understand that you have no idea what the word 'reservation' means."

"Okay, that's it, sir." Then she took a piece of paper, which Mark assumed was his reservation, and tore it in half, then threw it in the garbage can next to the desk. "There, you indeed DO NOT have a reservation with us any longer." Then, she turned around and walked back to her office. The other agent took a step back and said nothing.

The Redneck in Mark really wanted to jump out now. But the Irishman in Mark kept him under control. The agent finally said, "Next." Mark looked behind him and a young couple took a step backwards . . . just in case. Then, Mark walked away and saw a car rental company at the end of the aisle with no one in line, but the light was on. He had never heard of this company, but he walked up to the desk and a young girl smiled at him and said,

"Can I help you, sir?"

"Do you have any cars to rent?"

"We have a couple of cars left, not our newest models, but they are safe and reliable. Are you interested?"

"Yes, very interested. I need to get to Dungloe quickly."

She replied, "Dungloe? Is that in Ireland? I've never heard of it."

"Yes, it's in Ireland. Where else would it be."

"I'm just asking sir, no need to take that tone."

Mark took a deep breath and said, "I'm sorry, miss. My wife is having our baby and I really need to get to the hospital."

"Wait here, I'll be right back." She walked away and came back in less than a minute, holding a set of keys. She continued, "Let's get you to sign these papers and you can be on your way." Mark signed the documents, then ran out to the parking lot and went to the designated spot to find a beat up, dented, and very old Volkswagen Beetle waiting for him. He tried the key in the door, hoping it wouldn't open, but it did. He got in and the car started immediately. Mark pulled out of the lot and realized he didn't have a clue which way to go. Dublin was a big, congested, and very confusing place to drive in. After a few blocks of not knowing where he was, he spotted a taxi stand and pulled up behind a yellow cab.

The driver was standing outside, smoking a cigarette, and Mark walked up to him and said, "Sir, I'm completely lost and don't even know how to get out of Dublin. Can I hire you to lead me out of town? I'll follow you and pay you when we're out of the city."

The driver said, "Where are you going?"

"Dungloe, it's up north."

"I know where Dungloe is. Can I trust you to pay me?"

"Of course, you can."

"Then, let's go. Just follow me. Don't worry about any traffic signs, just stay behind me."

Mark said, "Okay." They turned here and there and back and forth, Mark had no idea where they were or where they were going, but after about twenty minutes of this, he could tell they were leaving the city. The driver then pulled over at a restaurant and Mark pulled in beside him and got out of the car. He thanked the driver, paid him a healthy sum, and followed his directions toward the main road to Galway. From there, he could find his way.

The old VW wasn't pretty, but it ran well. Mark drove on toward Galway, then followed the back roads on his way toward Dungloe. It was approximately a two-hour drive to Galway, then another two hours to Dungloe. Mark really needed to stop and visit a restroom, but he didn't. He thought he could make it all the way—he couldn't. Somewhere between Galway and Dungloe, as the road went through the lush fields and valleys, Mark waited until there was no car behind him, then he pulled over quickly and watered the heather. He jumped back in the car and took off again—no more stops until he reached the hospital.

THIRTY-EIGHT

THE LOCAL HOSPITAL WAS SMALL and nearly everyone there knew who Mark was, since he ran the most popular pub in town. When he rushed in the door, the receptionist instantly recognized him and said, "This way, sir." She led him down a long hallway, then up a short flight of stairs, and into a set of double doors labeled, "Delivery." She led Mark to a nurses' station and told them who he was, one of the nurses told him to follow her. She walked down to a small room, where they put a face mask on him, a surgical cap, a gown, and sanitary gloves.

When he was properly dressed, she took him down the hallway where he could hear a baby crying. He momentarily stopped and the nurse said, "She's yours." Mark almost fainted. He ran to the door that had the crying noise and slowly walked in. He saw Niamh holding a crying baby and staring down at it. He walked over to the bed, and she looked up at him and said, "Our baby girl, Mark, our baby. I knew you'd be here."

The baby was crying its little lungs out, however, when she opened her eyes and saw Mark staring down, somehow, she stopped crying and looked at Mark as though she was smiling at him. He leaned down and kissed Niamh, then leaned in and kissed his baby girl. He asked, "How long ago?"

Niamh answered, "Maybe five minutes, I'm not sure."

Then, one of nurses answered and said, "More like three minutes. Mother and daughter are fine." After several more minutes, or hours, or days—Mark wasn't sure—they let him sit and hold his baby girl. The most beautiful baby girl in the history of baby girls. Mickey Mantle, Michael Jordan, and King Henry VIII could have all walked in the room at that moment and Mark would have never seen them. He couldn't take his eyes off his girl . . . his and Niamh's baby girl.

He stayed all night at the hospital, while Niamh slept. She was totally exhausted after being in labor for over thirty-six hours. The little girl cried a little, but she mostly slept as well, usually in Mark's arms, as long as they would let him hold her. One of the nurses asked him what the baby's name was . . . he didn't know. They hadn't decided yet. Niamh had several names she had bantered about, hoping to get some sort of reaction from Mark. He didn't really care, as long as Niamh was happy. Mark thought about his mother's name, Shelley, and Niamh's mother's name, Casey, and Niamh's grandmother's name, Elizabeth, but again, he didn't care, as long as Niamh was happy.

The next morning, when Niamh was feeling better, she told Mark to go home and take a nap—he refused. He wanted to hold their baby as much as possible. The hospital staff informed them that they didn't have to decide on a name at that moment, they could wait a day or two. Mark stayed awake with excitement for over two days before the effects of sleeplessness overtook him. He was sitting next to Niamh as she was breastfeeding the baby and he simply nodded off. Niamh noticed and asked the nurse to recline the chair he was sitting in. She did that and then Niamh had one baby sleeping in her lap, and another baby sleeping in the chair next to her. She was in heaven.

That afternoon, Niamh's parents brought Ennis over to the hospital, Niamh's daughter with Gorden. When she walked in the room and saw her mother holding the baby, she cried out, "Mary!" She ran to the bed and hugged her mother's neck, woke up Mark and hugged his neck, and finally, gently leaned over, and kissed the baby's forehead.

Niamh then asked her, "Why did you say the name, 'Mary', when you walked in?"

"Because, Mom, she looks just like a Mary. Doesn't she?"

Mark chimed in and answered, "Yes, she does, Ennis. And if it's okay with your mom, Mary it will be." Niamh nodded, then started crying as all four members of the new family started hugging each other.

* * *

Little Mary was a strong baby, as evidenced by the loud crying sounds she could make. She certainly had a way of manipulating those around her to get what she wanted. When the new family, plus grandparents, arrived home, they all took turns holding Mary, feeding her, and ogling over her, because she was without a doubt, the prettiest, most precious baby ever born in the history of the world. That was undisputed. After a couple of weeks, Niamh took Mary down to the restaurant to meet Mark for lunch and introduce her to Claire. Claire insisted on holding the baby and feeding her a bottle while walking around the restaurant introducing her to everyone seated at the tables.

Then, they went to the pub, and Siobhan also had to hold her while showing her off to all the staff and customers. Mark's jaw soon started to ache from the constant and unavoidable smiling he was doing. Half the people that morning, thought Mary looked like Niamh, and the other half thought she looked like Mark. But all agreed she was the prettiest baby, in the history of babies, in all of Ireland.

Meanwhile, in Winston-Salem, Amie had her newborn son, Jacob, on display at Finnegan's for everyone to see. All who came in the pub also agreed that Jacob was the best-looking baby in the history of babies in North Carolina, if not the entire United States. Eric totally agreed!

And so . . . our trilogy ends. Mark and Niamh and Ennis and little Mary lived a fairytale life. Once the newness of the birth faded away, Claire once again began to be a constant pain in Mark's neck. Siobhan never said anything, but in her heart, she also wanted a beautiful baby like the one Mark and Niamh kept bringing around the pub. Eileen, who had moved to Paris, woke up one morning to the sound of a baby crying, even though there was no baby in her apartment. She laid in bed and thought, *congratulations, Mark, I hope you're happy.*

Jims threw a big party for the new parents at his pub in Burtonport. And a true miracle happened that night—old Conner didn't make any passes at Niamh, and even said a word in English, when he looked down at Mary and uttered, "Beautiful."

Eric and Amy could not wait to get started on baby #2, on their way to EIGHT. And the beautiful Gabriella tried her best to stay busy and active, even though her heart was irrevocably broken. There was only one Ailen that God ever made, and unfortunately, she knew that.

Desmond did buy the brewery and it made a nice profit for him and Stella each month, as did the new brewery that Ailen bought and started, which Eric operated, and Mark oversaw. Turns out that Winston-Salem could easily sustain multiple breweries, even two blocks apart.

And Mark . . . even though he loved Winston-Salem and would always be a southern hillbilly at heart, he was now an embedded Irishman. Linked to the valleys of green, the mist-covered hills, next to the cloudy coastlines, and leprechaun-ridden old castles scattered amongst the lakes and rainbows. And even though he was constantly spent from so many nights, up all sorts of hours feeding Mary, and the days arguing with Claire, and doing the paperwork for all the businesses in Dungloe and Winston-Salem, he was always smiling. Why? Because Mark knew that LOVE is what makes you smile, even when you're tired.

This, as with all my books, could not have been completed without the help of some special people. Editing, rereading, checking, fact-finding, and supporting is a lot of work. Mostly the kind of work I can't do. I'm too busy golfing, traveling, watching ballgames, and napping to do any of that hard stuff.

That's why I have PI and Larry. They do all the hard work. And I thank them from the bottom of my heart.

www.ingramcontent.com/pod-product-compliance
Lightning Source LLC
Chambersburg PA
CBHW041148250626
47164CB00015B/174